The Black Coat Script Library

America's Ace Spy-Swatter
A Five-Chapter Serial for Television
by
Gerry Conway & Roy Thomas

A Black Coat Press Book

Acknowledgements: We are indebted to Ted Fields, Brian K. Morris for retyping the typescript and David McDonnell for proofreading it.

Visit our website at www.blackcoatpress.com

ISBN 1-932983-22-8. First Printing. April 2005. Published by Black Coat Press, an imprint of Hollywood Comics.com, LLC, P.O. Box 17270, Encino, CA 91416. All rights reserved.

Introduction

By the early 1980s, Gerry Conway and I had already been in the comic book field for well over three decades between us–I since 1965, and he since 1968-69. Though we had each spent much of our comics careers to date writing for Marvel Comics, we were scripting for DC Comics when we teamed up to write and sell eight screenplays between 1981-85, two of which (*Fire and Ice* and *Conan the Destroyer*) actually got made into films in one form or another.

Doc Dynamo was born in a conference at Interscope, an independent production company in Westwood, California, run by Ted Fields (of the Marshall Fields family) who, around that time, had a big hit with *Revenge of the Nerds*. If my memory isn't playing tricks on me, it was Interscope producer Dave Obst–the same man who, as a demon literary agent, had represented Bob Woodward and Carl Bernstein's book *All the President's Men*, and in the mid-1970s, had sold DC and Marvel on the idea of a crossover between Superman and Spider-Man–who had this notion that it might be fun to do a send-up of oldtime movie serials.

Gerry and I sparked to that at once, as Gerry had loved watching them on TV–and I was actually old enough to have sat through many a one in actual movie theatres. The ultimate customer was supposedly going to be the Showtime network, with whom Interscope had an arrangement, though we never met with anyone from Showtime proper.

This screenplay was scripted to be divisible into five parts–like the chapters of one of the original serials, which usually had 12 or 15 of them. These five parts could later be gathered together to be shown as a feature, which would've been an hour and a half or so long. In addition, one of us had the (we thought) fiendishly clever idea that, in between weekly showings of the five individual chapters, viewers would be asked to vote (by phone or mail, in those innocent pre-Internet days) on two different ways the hero could get out of the cliffhanger predicament we'd left him at the close of the preceding chapter. Both solutions would have been filmed, of course, so that either one could be slugged in. (Hopefully, the feature version would've found a way to showcase both of them.)

Gerry and I had a ball doing the screenplay, although in the end, the execs at Showtime passed, to our and Interscope's disappointment. There was a later attempt to get *Doc Dynamo* going again with producer Dean Hargrove, who was quite enthusiastic about it. Alas, that came to naught, as well, although a couple of years later Gerry would do some of his first TV scripting for Dean on series like *The New Perry Mason* and others... while I contented myself with writing more of the super-hero comic books on which *Doc Dynamo* had been based in the first place. But I've never quite entirely given up my hope of seeing it produced...and it's fun to see it in print.

Roy Thomas

DOC DYNAMO

Doc Dynamo

FADE IN:

<u>TITLE CARD</u>: *"DOC DYNAMO - America's Ace Spy-Swatter."* Minimal credits, TRIUMPHAL MUSIC, follow by (ON A DOWN NOTE):

<u>TITLE CARD</u>: *"CHAPTER ONE: WHEELS OF DEATH!"*

WIPE TO:

<u>NEWSREEL LOGO (BLACK & WHITE) - *"MOVIETOWN NEWS"*</u>
The name itself in Art Deco letters. At bottom of screen, a pair of searchlights sweep the sky, amid MONTAGE of newsreel-style scenes of America at work and play. UPBEAT MUSIC behind it. This, and newsreel which follows, are in BLACK & WHITE.

<u>TITLE CARD</u> (WITH *MOVIETOWN NEWS* LOGO). It reads: *HITLER CONQUERS MAINLAND EUROPE! IS AMERICA NEXT?*

<u>MAP OF EUROPE</u> (AS PER EARLY 1940): Nazi Germany and conquered lands (Austria, Czechoslovakia, most of Poland) a darker color than rest of the continent. In midst of German area is a large black Swastika, in a white circle.

<u>SUPERED</u> at bottom: *1940.*

A husky male voice solemnly intones over DRAMATIC MARTIAL MUSIC.

NARRATOR (V.O.)
For the second time in this century, the European
continent is ravaged by the dogs of war. One by one,
nations have fallen prey to the fearsome fangs of
Adolf Hitler's Third Reich: Denmark... Norway...
Holland... Belgium... France... Luxembourg...

At each name there's a dramatic CLASH OF CYMBALS,
except that for tiny Luxembourg there is only the RINGING
OF A TINY, TINNY BELL. At the same time, the dark areas
of map expand, as if ink had been spilled on it. (Note: Only
"Vichy France" darkened, etc.)

MAP OF UNITED STATES, 1940.

NARRATOR (V.O.)
While, a vast ocean away, an America still at peace
begins at last to marshal its great natural resources–

MONTAGE (STOCK FOOTAGE): IMAGES in rapid succes-
sion of brawny steelworkers in busy steel mills... trains racing
along tracks... assembly-line factories turning out planes and
tanks... and famous rear-view pin-up of Betty Grable, all UN-
DER-SCORED NOW BY TRIUMPHAL MUSIC.

NARRATOR (V.O.)
–so that it may in truth become what President
Roosevelt has proudly proclaimed it–"The Arsenal
of Democracy!"

Abruptly, the TRIUMPHANT NEWSREEL MUSIC TURNS
SOUR...

NARRATOR (V.O.) (cont'd)
But now, without warning, the nation's burgeoning
defense industries are suddenly being crippled by an

> NARRATOR (V.O.) (cont'd)
> astonishing series of surprising acts of startling
> sabotage... which nobody expected!

NEWSREEL/IRIS MONTAGE (B&W STOCK FOOTAGE):
ACTS OF SABOTAGE. Again in rapid succession, images of
factories being blown up... trains being derailed... more factories blowing up... cargo ships sinking at sea... more factories
blowing up... trucks being hijacked... still more factories going
boom.

> NARRATOR (V.O.)
> In recent months, however, a new American cham-
> pion has arisen... one man who seems to succeed
> where even our police forces and J. Edgar Hoover's
> mighty FBI have failed...

A rippling American flag replaces the exploding factories...
and superimposed over the flag, the SHADOW OF DOC
DYNAMO in a heroic pose. DRAMATIC MUSIC SURGES
to a climax...

> NARRATOR (V.O.) (cont'd)
> ... the man of mystery known only as... Doc Dynamo,
> America's Ace Spy-Swatter!

> CROSS-WIPE CUT TO:

EXT. EMPIRE STATE BUILDING (1940) - DAY (STOCK)
SUPERED across bottom of screen: *AND, IN A CERTAIN
NAMELESS CITY...*

INT. WAITING ROOM OFFICE DOOR - DAY
On the outside of the opaque glass is printed: *DR. FRED
FRANKLIN, Pediatrician.* From within, we hear a LONG,
LOW DRONING "AHHHHH"...

INT. DR. FRED'S OFFICE - DAY

CLOSE on the gaping mouth of a gangly LITTLE GIRL (PEGGY) being invaded by a tongue depressor. She is saying "AHHHHH" in an afflicted tone of voice.

CAMERA PULLS BACK to reveal depressor held by Dr. Fred Franklin, who wrestles Peggy to keep the depressor in place as she kicks and struggles. He never loses his cheerful good will.

DR. FRED (early 30's) is tall, lean, rather Gary Cooperish, wearing the white smock of a pediatrician. He exudes confidence, competence, good will and honor. A man of few words, especially around women. He is also, secretly, DOC DYNAMO.

NURSE NANCY WALLACE (middle 20's, in nurse uniform and cap) is a direct young woman in Rosalind Russell mode, always ready with a quip and a smile. Loves Doc Dynamo, not Dr. Fred; he's too woman-shy to understand the difference.

>   DR. FRED
> Wider.

Peggy complies. As her mouth gets wider, her AHHH gets louder.

>   DR. FRED (cont'd)
> Wider...

Peggy opens still wider, and now her voice nearly deafens Nurse Nancy. Dr. Fred remains happily immune.

>   DR. FRED (cont'd)
> That's fine, Peggy. You may close your mouth now.

She does–biting the depressor in two with a LOUD SNAP! Without missing a beat, Dr. Fred delicately retrieves the remainder of his sundered depressor and drops it in a wastebasket.

> DR. FRED (cont'd)
> I'll just toss this one away.

> NANCY
> There, that wasn't so bad, was it?

Peggy delivers a swift kick toward Dr. Fred's shin; he narrowly avoids it and chuckles benignly. Nancy gives him an exasperated, long-suffering look.

> DR. FRED
> Careful, Peggy. I know you didn't mean to, but you nearly kicked me that time.

> NANCY
> Really, Dr. Fred–do you have to let every child that comes in here get away with murder?

> DR. FRED
> Oh, now, Nurse Wallace, there's no need to exaggerate...

Peggy kicks again, taking him in the shin, as she runs out of the room. Fred hops backward, still smiling.

The waiting room door opens behind Dr. Fred, and he collides with POLICE INSPECTOR ARTHUR "ACE" BURLINGTON (early 30's).

ANGLE - ACE
is a somewhat off-center and well-meaning buffoon, who tries to model himself after Dick Tracy, down to the snap-brim hat

and two-way wrist radio. In his case, the radio is an unwieldy walkie-talkie strapped to his forearm. Ace carries a not-very-well-hidden torch for Nurse Nancy, who can't see him for dust.

> ACE
> (disentangling)
> Hey, take it easy with those fancy dance-steps, Dr. Fred. Or have you changed your last name to As-taire?

Ace chuckles at his little joke. Dr. Fred stands up straight, smiling, still favoring his sore shin.

> DR. FRED
> Oh, hello, Police Inspector Burlington. What brings you here?

> ACE
> Actually, Nurse Wallace—Nancy—I'm here to see you.

> NANCY
> (trying to look busy)
> Me?

Ace smirks at Nancy, leans against a tabletop with a debonair air... and knocks over a whole glassful of tongue depressors. Dr. Fred retrieves them with a sigh, and cheerfully dumps them in the wastebasket, as Ace tries to hit on Nancy.

> DR. FRED
> I'll just toss these 25 away...

> ACE
> (continuing over)
> Here I am, all set to leave for Long Island on impor-tant police business—top secret hush hush, y'know,

ACE (cont'd)
practically government stuff–and I suddenly remem-
bered I don't have a date for the Defense Bond Rally
tonight.

NANCY
Sounds tempting, Inspector...

ACE
Call me Ace. All my first-time offenders do.

She's groping for words when, on the desk, a glass container
full of lollipops begins blinking on and off. Nancy sees the
blinking lollipop jar and quickly edges around to block it from
Ace's view.

NANCY
...but I have to stay late tonight and help Dr. Fred
with his four o'clock appointment.
(raises voice slightly)
Don't I, Dr. Fred?

DR. FRED
(looks up, puzzled)
My four o'clock appointment?

NANCY
You know. With the man from the Big White House.

A bit exasperated with Dr. Fred, Nancy winks, gestures with
her chin, winks. Dr. Fred finally notices the blinking jar and
raises his eyebrows, making an "oh" expression. He backs
toward his inner sanctum, all smiles and apologies.

DR. FRED
Sorry to rush off like this, Inspector–

                            ACE
        Ace.

                          DR. FRED
        Ace–but duty calls. We mustn't ignore the little
        things of life, must we?

Dr. Fred chuckles benignly and ducks through the door
marked: *PRIVATE*. Burlington shakes his head, looks back at
Nancy.

                            ACE
        You got class, sister. I don't figure you for hanging
        around with a loser like Franklin. Or is it somebody
        else you're really stuck on?

                          NANCY
                 (looking toward inner door)
        It's... someone else. Sort of.

INT. DOC'S INNER SANCTUM - DAY
Dr. Fred, the door shut behind him, pulls a shade down over
the frosted glass. The room is furnished entirely in black and
white, austere, Art Deco on the modernistic side. Dr. Fred
goes to a black wardrobe and throws it open to reveal–

THE COSTUME
There, gleaming in the light, are the white aviator's helmet
and goggles, the white scarf, the white flight-suit, the white
leather gloves and boots, of Doc Dynamo. On the back of the
flight suit is a stylized drawing of a dynamo, crossed by a
lightning bolt. DRAMATIC MARTIAL MUSIC.

INT. DR. FRED'S OFFICE
Ace studies his own reflection in the glass of the door marked
PRIVATE.

                            16

ACE

OK, OK. I can take anything but a hint. But you're making a mistake. Ace Burlington is on his way up in the police department. I'm going to be the next Dick Tracy. Lookit my two-way walkie-talkie.

Holds up his wrist.

NANCY

You must have a strong wrist. Maybe some other time.

ACE
(grins)
It's a date. See you later, crime-stopper.

Adjusting his hat with what he thinks is a rakish gesture, Ace leaves, closing the front door behind him. Nancy, drained, gives a sigh of relief.

INT. DOC'S INNER SANCTUM - CLOSE - DOC DYNAMO'S TELE-VISOR
A large TV-like screen on one wall, with lots of buttons around, above, below it. A MILKY IMAGE takes form on screen–solidifying to show (in black-and-white, of course) FRANKLIN DELANO ROOSEVELT and his lap-terrier Fala, seated before a window through which we see the Washington Monument.

FDR

My good friend... Once again, your country needs you. I need you.

FDR is puffing at cigarette in his cigarette holder. His dog makes a YIPPING BARK. CAMERA PULLS BACK to reveal Dr. Fred, now in his Doc Dynamo outfit, adjusting the goggles of his flight helmet.

DOC DYNAMO

stands in a dramatic pose, hands on hips, smile on his face. A breeze from nowhere blows his scarf at a horizontal angle. In this identity, Dr. Fred has a deeper voice, and moves with the pantherish grace and cockiness of the fearless masked aviator and adventurer he really is; he hardly seems the same person.

> DOC
>
> Doc Dynamo reporting, ready for action,
> Mr. President.

> FDR
>
> Excellent. Because the mission I have for you this time is one which may decide whether the United States of America survives the next few years—or whether our nation, too, falls victim to the Nazi juggernaut.

> DOC
>
> You know which way I vote on that one, sir.

> FDR
>
> Doc, have you ever hear of—the Keppler Rocketplane?

DRAMATIC DRUMBEAT. As FDR talks, he holds several photographs in sequence up to the Tele-Visor lens, pictures of the Icarus Aircraft Company factory, of Dr. Hans Keppler and of the Rocketplane engine.

> FDR (cont'd)
>
> It seems fantastic, I know. But with the help of the good Americans over at Icarus Aircraft Company, Dr. Hans Keppler, the world-famous Swiss scientist, has developed the prototype engine for a fantastic airplane to be powered by mighty rockets...

                    FDR (cont'd)
With Dr. Keppler's amazing new engine, the Rocketplane will be capable of achieving far greater speeds
than any current aircraft.

The last photograph is a cartoon showing the Rocketplane
zooming past a slow-moving Army Air Force prop fighter.

                    DOC
Won't all those rockets melt the propeller?

                    FDR
The Rocketplane doesn't need a propeller, Doc.

                    DOC
            (startled, thoughtful)
    I... see.

INT. DR. FRED'S OFFICE - NANCY
straightening up a shelf, as a sinister shadow falls over her.
Suddenly, touches her shoulder. She jumps. She turns angrily
on her kid brother, RICKY, who grins sheepishly. Ricky is a
freckled, red-headed Mickey Rooney at 13 going on 40.

                    RICKY
Hi, sis! Did I scare you?

                    NANCY
I thought you were at the pictures.

                    RICKY
Aw, that stuff's for kids. I want some real excite-
ment. You know—like Dr. Fred has when he puts on
that outfit and becomes—you know. *Him.*

NANCY

Ricky, I've told you a hundred times, Dr. Fred is just a humble pediatrician.

RICKY
(winking)
Sure he is.

Sighing, she picks up her purse and counts out some change.

NANCY

How much?

RICKY
There's a great double-feature down at the Roxy...
Gene Autry and Sunset Carson. Call it two bits.
(takes the money)
Gee, thanks, sis! You're a wiz!

He goes out as Nancy shakes her head and looks wistfully toward the door marked PRIVATE.

INT. DOC'S INNER SANCTUM
Doc studies the Tele-Visor image of the Rocketplane engine.

DOC
Quite a tempting target for Fifth Column saboteurs.

FDR
Isn't it? What's more, we've received reports that Hitler has ordered his top spy in America to steal or destroy every American secret weapon. A deadly, hooded spy we know only as–*The Thunder*.

OMINOUS RUMBLING makes Doc look up, as if expecting rain.

FDR (cont'd)
Well, Doc... can I count on you to protect the Rocketplane?

DOC
With my dying breath, Mr. President.

FDR
Let's hope that won't be necessary. This is your
Commander-in-Chief, signing off.
(Fala yips)
Yes, and Fala, too.

Picture goes back to test pattern and the usual annoying
WHINE. Doc turns off the set, then turns dramatically TO-
WARD CAMERA, which ZEROES IN on him.

INT. DR. FRED'S OFFICE – NANCY
looks up as the private office door swings open, tangling
briefly on the still-drawn shade. The shade snaps up and Doc
Dynamo strides dramatically into the room. Nancy reacts like
a girl with a painfully obvious schoolgirl crush–as if Doc
really is a different person from Dr. Fred. Her voice is full of
hero worship mixed with desire.

NANCY
Doc Dynamo!

DOC
I think you'd best cancel all of Dr. Fred's appoint-
ments for the rest of the day, Nurse Wallace.

She rushes to him, puts her head against his shoulder. Doc
cringes away but bucks up and takes it like a man.

NANCY
Oh, Doc... You will be careful, won't you?

                    NANCY (cont'd)
Sometimes I get so worried for you when you're out
fighting all those gangsters and counterfeiters and
saboteurs...
                    (grins, pulls away to give him a
                    playful sock on the jaw)
Why do you do it, anyway?

                    DOC
It's what he would have wanted.

He glances at a portrait on the wall–a tall, handsome man with
greying hair, enough like Dr. Fred Franklin to be his father.

                    DOC (cont'd)
I've never told you this... but Dad was the original
Doc Dynamo.

He flips the portrait around–another portrait on the back shows
Doc's father wearing the Dynamo costume, an identical pose.

                    DOC (cont'd)
Dad gave his life fighting for justice, freedom and
human dignity. I'm just carrying on his fight.
                    (awkwardly)
Nancy–I mean, Nurse Wallace... I...

He swallows, looks away–looks back, smiles wistfully, play-
fully socks her jaw. Her head snaps around from the force of
the blow.

                    NANCY
                    (recovering)
Go on, you big lug. Go make the world safe for democracy.

He goes out, with a grin. She collapses back against the desk, rubbing her jaw, eyes wide. But she still looks adoringly at the door through which he just exited, sighing.

INT. EMPIRE STATE BUILDING GARAGE - DAY
Doc crosses deserted garage to a long, low-slung convertible roadster covered by a white car-shroud. Pulls shroud away to reveal (with dramatic FANFARE ON SOUND): WHITE LIGHTNING, the most powerful automobile in existence in 1940, a gleaming, shining, glowing machine–all white. The license plate reads: *DYNAMO*. On each side of the car are emblazoned the words *WHITE LIGHTNING* skewered on a thunderbolt.

As Doc swings easily over the side of the car and slips behind the wheel, Ricky runs INTO VIEW from his hiding place behind a pillar. Ricky heads for the rear of White Lightning, unseen by Doc.

RICKY
climbs into the trunk and pulls the lid down firmly behind him.

WHITE LIGHTNING
zooms across the garage with a ROAR of mighty pistons–and out onto the street.

EXT. MIDTOWN MANHATTAN STREET - DAY - (STOCK) (1940)

INSERT - CORNERSTONE
The name reads: *ICARUS AIRCRAFT BUILDING*. And, carved in smaller letters below: *THE SKY IS OUR LIMIT*.

DISSOLVE TO:

INT. ICARUS BOARDROOM - HARRY LANTON - DAY

sits at head of an otherwise unseen conference table, a huge picture window behind him through which a skyscraper backdrop can be seen. A metal nameplate in front of Lanton reads: *HARRY LANTON, PRESIDENT.*

Lanton is a distinguished-looking, 50-ish Lew Ayres type, with pencil-thin moustache and slicked-back greying hair. He speaks confidently.

>   LANTON
> Well, Al? Is the Rocketplane engine prototype ready
> for its final test tomorrow morning?

CLOSE - AL PALMER

This burly Alan Hale type bangs his big fist on the table–something he does, as it turns out, nearly every time he speaks. (Even upsets nameplate reading "ALVIN 'AL' PALMER, Chief Engineer.") A direct, no-nonsense type, his coat slung over his chair, shirt-sleeves rolled up to reveal brawny, hairy arms.

>   PALMER
> I'll say this, Mr. Lanton–the Engineering Department
> will do its part! You can count on that! That rocket
> engine'11 work tomorrow, and this war will be over
> in a couple of months–tops!

>   LANTON
> Chislewit? Does our chief accountant have anything
> to add?

CHISLEWIT

Behind his *"MARTIN CHISLEWIT, Chief Accountant"* nameplate sits a young Vincent Price type, diffident yet suspicious of everyone.

CHISLEWIT
Only that Icarus Aircraft is $20 million in the red so
far on the development of the Keppler Rocketplane
engine–
          (a mildly reproachful
          look in Keppler's direction)
–and that, if it fails, the whole company will doubt-
less go into bankruptcy.
          (beat)
Also that the time expended at this board meeting has
run up costs by another $3789 and 17 cents.

He sits back smugly.

DR. KEPPLER
seated behind nameplate reading *"DR. HANS KEPPLER,
Chief Designer."* A Swiss emigré who resembles a more in-
tellectual Peter Lorre, Keppler is anxious, sensitive about his
invention and background.

                    KEPPLER
Money, schmoney. Mein Rocketplane is so advanced,
it will make var impossible for a thousand years, give
or take a century. I have just von question, Mr. Lanton.

BOARDROOM
For the first time, we see that the conference table around
which the men sit is very long, with a huge amount of space
between any two men. Every man in the room is dressed in an
identical double-breasted suit.

                    KEPPLER (cont'd)
Vot about dis top Nazi spy ve keep hearing rumors
about–der von called Der Thunder?

LANTON

Rumors, Dr. Keppler? What rumors?

From under the table, Keppler piles a bunch of magazines and newspapers onto it: *TIME, NEWSWEEK, SATURDAY EVENING POST, BETTER HOMES & GARDENS.*

On each cover a picture of THE THUNDER, in full regalia, with identical headings: *THE THUNDER–TOP NAZI SPYMASTER!* Keppler next plunks down a copy of the *NEW YORK GLOBE-WORLD-STAR-HERALD-JOURNAL*, whose headline reads: *THE THUNDER VOWS TO CAPTURE OR DESTROY EVERY AMERICAN SECRET WEAPON!*

LANTON

Oh, *those* rumors.
(with a superior smile)
Gentlemen, I have a surprise announcement to make.
I have spoken personally with President Roosevelt,
and he has assigned his most trusted special agent to
protect the engine prototype.
(aside)
Did you get all that, Hooper?

HOOPER

Oh yes, most certainly, Mr. Lanton, sir.

Seated on an uncomfortable folding chair is STANLEY HOOPER, the Board's secretary, a fussy little nobody in a grey suit, barely five feet tall if he stood up–as inoffensive as Wally Cox. He checks a notepad on his lap, prissily and efficiently.

LANTON

Members of the board, may I present–
(looong dramatic pause)
... Doc Dynamo!

Lanton looks at the door. Nothing. He clears his throat nervously... and suddenly, Doc comes swinging on a cable line through the picture window, SHATTERING the glass far and wide. Lanton, Hooper and the Board members all react in surprise.

Doc releases the line, deftly brushes a few slivers of glass off his outfit and strides (SOUND OF CRUNCHING GLASS under his boots) to Lanton, who rises.

> LANTON
> I must say, Doc, you make a colorful entrance.

> DOC
> In my line of work, Mr. Lanton, the element of surprise is essential. And because surprise is essential if I'm to succeed in stopping The Thunder...

An ominous RUMBLING OF THUNDER outside interrupts him...

> DOC (cont'd)
> ... no one outside this room must know that I've been assigned to this project. Otherwise, my life–and those of my operatives–would be severely endangered.

CAMERA PANS around the table from Lanton past Hooper in background to each of the members. Each nods, MURMURS "Of course... of course..." but then looks shifty-eyed at the next man, back around to Lanton.

> LANTON
> Doc, you have the collective word of the finest executive board money can buy.

                    PALMER
               (pounding fist on table)
    Mr. Lanton, I know I speak for each of us when I say
    we'll all breathe just a little easier tonight, knowing
    Doc Dynamo is on the job!

More AUDIBLE MURMUR.

                    CHISLEWIT
               (whispering to Lanton)
    Er—he doesn't have to go on our payroll, does he?

Lanton gives Chislewit a cold look. Doc is oblivious.

                    DOC
    And now, gentlemen, I know you must get ready for
    tomorrow's test, so I'll take my leave.

The Board members all turn toward the window, expecting
Doc to swing back out. But Doc simply strides to the door,
opens it and steps out, closing it quietly behind him.

                    LANTON
    Gentlemen, until tomorrow morning, this meeting
    stands adjourned.

Lanton BANGS his gavel and, amid GENERAL MURMUR,
all five men file out boardroom door, as CAMERA PANS
away from them to settle on a portrait of George Washington
over the mantle. There is the SOUND OF THE DOOR
SLAMMING. Slowly, the CAMERA PANS back toward the
door—which now opens as THE THUNDER enters furtively.

ANGLE - THE THUNDER
is of more than average height, his features hidden by a full
hood and flowing robe, both black—your standard serial-villain
issue, circa 1940—an image of a thundercloud emblazoned on

front of robe. He strides to the mantle, turns George upside down–and fireplace opens a wide crack, allowing The Thunder, after a glance behind him, to enter a secret chamber behind it.

INT. THE THUNDER'S SECRET CHAMBER - DAY
A stark, windowless room. The Thunder strides to a TV-like screen on far wall. Lots of knobs, dials, etc. He turns these as if it made a difference, and a Swastika Test Pattern appears, followed by the black-and-white image of Adolf Hitler. The Thunder's VOICE IS ALTERED AND AMPLIFIED by a futuristic-looking radio-speaker on a chain around his neck, as he gives the Nazi salute.

> THUNDER
> Heil Hitler! Mein Fuhrer, I must inform you that the final test of the Keppler Rocketplane engine prototype has been scheduled for tomorrow morning.

> HITLER
> We must have that engine! If we get that engine, my Third Reich will live a thousand years. If we don't get it, I'm not making any predictions.
> (rising anger)
> Get it! At any cost, do you hear?

> THUNDER
> (clicks heels with a clang)
> I will steal the Rocketplane engine this very night!

> HITLER
> Do not fail me, Thunder. Never forget... I'm your Fuhrer! Seig Heil!

He gives a salute as image fades. The Thunder turns toward the audience and glares malevolently TOWARD CAMERA, as it ZOOMS IN on him, amid DRAMATIC MUSIC.

IRIS WIPE TO:

EXT. ICARUS AIRCRAFT FACTORY - NIGHT
Several large buildings and an aircraft hangar rise in the middle of nowhere, surrounded by a 20-foot-high chain-link fence topped by barbed wire. The only road passes through a gate protected by a uniformed GUARD. A sign beside the gate reads: *ICARUS AIRCRAFT – TOP SECRET – NO SOLICITORS.*

EXT. DIRT ROAD - WHITE LIGHTNING - DUSK
parks behind several boulders, a hundred feet from the gate.

INT. WHITE LIGHTNING'S TRUNK
In darkness, Ricky hugs his knees, thrilled, mumbling to himself.

                    RICKY
          Oh boy, this is great!

EXT. WHITE LIGHTNING - DOC
at the wheel, puts an ungainly-looking pair of white thick-rimmed glasses over his goggles. He presses a button and the glasses telescope outward, into a pair of binoculars.

EXT. FACTORY BUILDING - DOC'S POV (BINOCULARS) - DUSK
A uniformed Guard on duty outside the main entrance, two SNARLING DOBERMANS on leashes beside him. Ace Burlington and Al Palmer approach the entrance, talking, though their voices can't be heard at this distance.

EXT. WHITE LIGHTNING – DOC
lowers the binoculars, grinning, unstraps seat belt. He reaches for a prominent red button on dashboard marked ejector, and pushes it. With an EXPLOSIVE HYDRAULIC *WHOOSH!*,

the driver's seat propels Doc straight up into the air like a circus acrobat shot from a cannon.

TRAVELING SHOT - DOC
somersaults in mid-air–pulling a ripcord from a jacket pocket. The dynamo-patch on the back of his flight jacket pops apart, a small parafoil-like parachute springing into the air.

INT. FACTORY COMPOUND - DOC
suspended under parachute, glides over fence and drops lightly to the ground on other side. Landing, he twists the ripcord again–and parachute retracts back into flight jacket, dynamo-patch sealing shut automatically. He smiles like a kid whose toy train works like a charm, heads across compound toward the main building.

INT. WHITE LIGHTNING'S TRUNK - RICKY
listens hard, then tries to open the trunk door.

EXT. WHITE LIGHTNING - TRUNK LID - CLOSE
jiggles–but doesn't open. MUFFLED VOICES from inside the trunk.

                    RICKY'S VOICE
          Oh, spit!

Suddenly, a shadow falls across the trunk... and an UNIDENTIFIED FIGURE crosses INTO VIEW, moving to the front of the car.

                    RICKY'S VOICE (cont'd)
          Doc! Hey, Doc–let me out of here!

THE FRONT HOOD - TWO SLENDER FEMALE HANDS
raise the hood, exposing the engine. One hand brings a small glass vial INTO FRAME, the other hand pulls stopper from

vial. A SMOKING GREEN LIQUID pours out over the tangle of wires inside engine.

WIRES SIZZLE and smolder, dissolving under acid's effect. The hands close the hood, and toss the vial away... but not before we get a glimpse of sleek, silk-stockinged female thigh.

The VIAL SMASHES against a rock, GREEN LIQUID SIZZLING, smoking.

The Figure slips away from the WHITE LIGHTNING... as Ricky's muffled voice comes from within trunk, plaintively:

> RICKY'S VOICE
> Aw, rats. Now I'm gonna miss everything.

INT. MAIN FACTORY BUILDING - DUSK
The catwalked interior echoes with Palmer and Ace's voices and FOOTSTEPS as they cross to a huge metal vault.

> PALMER
> Electric fences, guards and guard dogs, one of the most sophisticated alarm systems this side of Fort Knox... Like I told you, Inspector, we've taken every possible precaution to prevent anyone stealing the Rocketplane.

Above, a skylight opens, and Doc slides INTO VIEW. He drops to the catwalk, peers over edge. Chains dangle from the catwalk.

DOC'S POV - ACE & PALMER

> ACE
> There are spies and fifth columnists everywhere, Palmer. You can't be too careful.

Palmer stops before an oversize Van de Graf generator with globe-topped poles set on either side of the vault door.

> PALMER
> Even if an intruder did get this far... he'd never make it past our final defense.

Palmer throws a switch–an ELECTRIC ARC CRACKLES between the two poles, HISSING AND SIZZLING. From a bowl of fruit atop generator, Palmer takes an apple, tosses it to Ace... who takes a bite, then throws it into the arc. It DISINTEGRATES!

> PALMER (cont'd)
> Sixty thousand volts. Quite a fish fry.

Doc smiles, impressed.

Palmer shuts off the arc, then turns huge wheel lock controlling vault door. The door swings open with a GROAN OF HEAVY MACHINERY–

INT. VAULT
Palmer and Ace enter. It's empty, except for a glass display case in the center. Inside case, gleaming silver, the size of a large rocking horse, the Rocketplane engine prototype is streamlined and futuristic–like something off the cover of *Astounding Stories*.

> ACE
> Good gravy!

> PALMER
> (a proud parent)
> Beautiful, isn't she? The Keppler Rocketplane Engine... the only one of its kind in the world, or anywhere else!

Palmer bangs his fist on the glass for emphasis, cracking it.

                    PALMER (cont'd)
        Would you like a demonstration?

Ace nods eagerly, and Palmer swings open the cracked display
case to expose the Rocketplane's controls.

EXT. FACTORY GATE - GATE GUARD - DUSK
The GUARD watches as a battered old canvas-backed
TRUCK HISSES TO A STOP outside the gate, engine smoking. An OLD WOMAN climbs down from passenger side; a
beautiful YOUNG WOMAN in a tight dress (slit up one leg)
gets out on driver's side. They fuss with hood as the Guard
walks over, ogling the Young Woman–whose impossibly long
legs would catch any man's eye. The Old Woman angrily
swacks the engine block with a wrench.

                    OLD WOMAN
        Oh, darn! Now we'll never get all our scrap metal to
        town in time to help out the defense effort!

                    GUARD
        Need any help?

The Young Woman simpers at him, and the Guard grins at
her–crossing his eyes as the Old Woman belts him with the
wrench.

                    OLD WOMAN
        Not anymore we don't.

She pulls off her shawl to reveal "she" is really a "he"–
SHORTIE, one of The Thunder's gang. Young Woman
(GAMS CATLING) pulls a wired microphone from her garter
belt, exposing a familiar length of sleek, silk-stockinged thigh.
She speaks into it as the third gang member, LONGJOHN,

speaks into it as the third gang member, LONGJOHN, jumps from the rear of the truck and runs to help Shortie pull open the gate.

> GAMS
>
> Gams Catling to The Thunder. We're on our way.

She gets in, drives the truck through the opening gate. Shortie and Longjohn jump onto the running boards as the truck drives past.

> IRIS WIPE TO:

INT. MAIN FACTORY BUILDING - CLOSE ON ROCK-ETPLANE ENGINE
as it ROARS TO LIFE, SHOOTING a jet of flame 15 feet across the factory floor. CAMERA PULLS BACK to show Palmer has moved the engine out of the vault to give it more room to fire; he and Ace watch from one side, wearing welder's masks to protect their eyes. They have to shout to be heard over the ROARING JET FLAME.

> PALMER
>
> With an engine like this to propel it, the Rocketplane may eventually attain speeds of 400, even 500 miles an hour!

> ACE
>
> (startled)
> Can human beings live at such a speed?

> PALMER
>
> We're working on it.

Doc watches from above. Flame dies as Palmer cuts the controls.

ACE
Well, I've gotta admit, you're well protected, all right. You've certainly put my mind at rest.

Gam's voice comes from O.S., in direction of main entrance.

GAMS (O.S.)
Make one move, copper, and I'll put the rest of you to rest... permanently.

Doc reacts, glancing over–

DOC'S POV - GAMS, SHORTIE & LONGJOHN
in doorway with sub-machine guns in hand. Gams strikes a match on her sleek, silk-stockinged thigh and lights a small cigar.

GAMS
Shortie, Longjohn. You know what The Thunder wants. Go get it.

SHORTIE
Right, Gams.

Burlington and Palmer put up their hands as Shortie and Longjohn run toward them.

ACE
Gams Catling and her mob, eh? So now you've thrown in with traitors and saboteurs. Where's your sense of patriotic duty?

SHORTIE
We left it in Leavenworth, copper.

He pushes past Ace to get at the Rocketplane engine–but Ace grabs him in a bear hug.

SHORTIE (cont'd)
Longjohn, get his flatfoot offa' me!

Palmer backs up, unnoticed, ducks behind the vault, as Longjohn picks Ace up by the collar and starts to swing him
around–when there's a RATTLING SOUND from above.
Shortie, Longjohn and Ace all look up, gape-jawed, to see:

Doc Dynamo swings down INTO THE SCENE on one of the
dangling chains–RATTLING! AND CHINGING! He lets go–
and CRASHES into Ace, Shortie and Longjohn, feet first.

All fall in a tangle except Doc, who rolls away with an acrobat's grace, rebounding to his feet like a gymnast.

                    SHORTIE
        Holy Cow–

                    ACE
        It's–

                    GAMS
                (almost swooning)
        –Doc Dynamo!

Doc, in a dramatic pose, fists cocked. Sudden GUNFIRE
CHOPS UP the floor at his feet as Gams recovers her compo-
sure and BLASTS away. Doc makes an impossible leap–grabbing overhead chains and swinging above the GUNFIRE.

He lands, rolling, and ducks behind engine prototype. BUL-
LETS STOP when they near the engine.

                    SHORTIE
        What's the matter with you, boss? Shoot him!

GAMS
Can't take the chance! I might hit the engine! You get him!

Shortie and Longjohn do a take, then gulp and charge.

THE FIGHT
Doc uses the engine to block Shortie and Longjohn, finally swinging one end around into Longjohn's face, and ducking under it as the engine continues to swing about, narrowly missing Shortie. Shortie kicks at Doc's feet, Doc grabs one of Shortie's ankles and tosses him over. Gams, who's been watching, FIRES a short burst over Doc's head, sending him diving for cover.

Doc hits the ground palms first and manages to spring backward like someone on a trampoline. Somersaulting in mid-air, he lands on top of the Rocketplane engine.

THE VAULT (BEHIND ACE) - A SHADOWY FIGURE comes INTO VIEW–it's The Thunder, lurking near the generator. Ace doesn't see him–and The Thunder knocks him out with a gun butt. The Thunder watches the fight a moment, looks around at the generator–and pulls the lever, activating it. Sparks jump as electricity arcs between the two globe-topped poles.

THE FIGHT
Longjohn, clutching his face, still stunned from being walloped by the engine, backs up and steps on Shortie's hand. Shortie screams and yanks away, bumping into engine, which again spins around–this time throwing Doc off his feet. Doc falls forward–into Longjohn's waiting hands.

Longjohn gets Doc in throttling grip, lifting him off the floor–backs Doc toward the SIZZLING ELECTRIC ARC across vault door. Doc looks back, sees arc, tries to break free; hands pound uselessly against Longjohn's wrists. They get nearer and nearer the arc.

Doc–inches from the arc now–manages to bring knee up into Longjohn's groin, breaking his grip. Longjohn drops him, howling, and Doc stumbles back for balance–directly into the arc. ELECTRICITY HALOES him for seconds, as Longjohn limps away.

EXT. MAIN FACTORY ENTRANCE
The Thunder with Shortie's and Gams' help, pushes the engine out the entrance to the waiting truck.

The uniformed Guard lies unconscious by door, dogs limp beside him, jaws clamped on the steak. Parked behind the truck is the Thunderwagon, The Thunder's powerful automobile. This hardtop is a larger, bulkier-looking car than White Lightning, and has cloud insignia painted on the side.

THUNDER
Hurry. I'll follow in–The Thunderwagon!

THUNDER RUMBLES O.S.

INT. MAIN FACTORY
Ace stirring awake, sees Doc–instantly jumps to generator controls, shutting the arc down. Doc crashes, face forward, onto the ground. Ace bends over Doc. Doc opens his eyes–groggily gets up.

ACE
Sixty thousand volts, and you're alive?

DOC
Special rubber-soled boots.

EXT. FACTORY GATE
Thunder's Truck speeds through gate, churning up dust, heads up the road, followed at high speed by the Thunderwagon. The Thunderwagon's ENGINE RUMBLES LIKE THUNDER.

Doc runs INTO VIEW behind the disappearing vehicles, coughing from dust, wiping it from goggles–does a take, hurries toward where White Lightning is hidden.

CROSS-WIPE TO:

EXT. MOUNTAIN ROAD - NIGHT
Headlights spearing the darkness, truck and Thunder-wagon speed into a hairpin turn on a narrow two-lane mountain highway.

TRUCK CAB
Gams at wheel, Shortie and Longjohn jostling for position beside her. Shortie watches a side mirror, where a dim distant glow can be seen getting closer.

THUNDERWAGON
Thunder at the wheel. He glances at his own rearview mirror– that glow's a pair of headlights. He takes a large microphone from his dashboard.

WHITE LIGHTNING
ROARS by, in hot pursuit of The Thunder and his mob. Doc at the wheel, grim.

INT. TRUCK
Ricky jiggled and bumped, having the time of his life.

RICKY
Wow, wait'll the gang hears about this!

INT. TRUCK CAB
The Thunder's voice comes over a dashboard RADIO SPEAKER.

                    THUNDER (O.S.)
          Gams... Doc Dynamo is still alive!

                    GAMS
               (into her own mike)
          Not for long. I fixed his brakes. Another one of these
          hairpin turns, and no more White Lightning, no more
          Doc Dynamo!
               (sighs)
          Too bad... he sure was a looker.

Shortie starts laughing. Longjohn joins in. Gams gives them a look. They laugh louder and louder and louder–

EXT. MOUNTAIN ROAD
The truck speeds by, LAUGHTER DOPPLERING IN AND OUT. The THUNDERWAGON RUMBLES after it. Seconds later, White Lightning follows, WHEELS SCREECHING to make a sharp turn.

Doc at the wheel of White Lightning, grim.

Ricky in the trunk, whooping with delight.

Thunder and his Mob, cackling with laughter to the point of tears.

THE ROAD
More turns. Sharper and sharper. Dust and gravel shoot in all directions as first truck, then White Lightning, careen through torturous mountain doglegs.

WHITE LIGHTNING
Doc sees a sharp, almost 90-degree turn coming up ahead: the truck, pinned in his headlights, barely makes the turn, skidding through it. Doc puts his foot down on the brake.

THE BRAKE
Doc's foot hits the brake–and goes flat to the floor.

Doc reacts, trying brake again–but it's dead. The turn ahead looms like a sentence of death. Doc looks around, makes decision, starts to clamber up onto seat, ready to jump–and freezes with shock as he hears RICKY'S MUFFLED VOICE calling from the trunk:

> RICKY'S VOICE
> Hey, Doc–some fun, huh?!

Doc reacts with horror, then glances over his shoulder at:

DOC'S POV - THE CLIFF AHEAD
It looms, closer and closer, in the headlights–a veritable chasm, marked by a sign on a post: DANGER–DEAD MAN'S CURVE!

Doc–eyes wide behind his goggles–almost paralyzed with indecision.

> NARRATOR
> Can Doc free Ricky from the trunk in time? Or should he save himself, and jump? You decide!

> WIPE TO:

EXT. WHITE LIGHTNING - NIGHT
as the car rushes toward the precipice, Doc clings to the trunk, feverishly trying to free the latch.

NARRATOR
Should Doc Dynamo risk his own life to save Ricky?

SUPERED LEGEND ON SCREEN: *CHOICE #1: SAVE RICKY?*

WIPE TO:

EXT. WHITE LIGHTNING - NIGHT
as the car rushes toward the precipice, Doc leaps from the driver's seat into the darkness.

NARRATOR
Or should he save himself–and jump?

SUPERED LEGEND ON SCREEN: *CHOICE #2: OR JUMP?*

WIPE TO:

EXT. MOUNTAIN ROAD - NIGHT
A spectacular view of White Lightning CRASHING through guard rail, in long, graceful arc out into the night!

NARRATOR
To learn what answer you choose, tune in next week for the second thrilling episode of *"Doc Dynamo"*!

As the NARRATOR'S VOICE CONCLUDES ON SOUND, the SUPERED TITLE: *"Don't Miss CHAPTER TWO: FLAM-ING DOOM!"* appears across the screen, burning through the film as we...

FADE OUT.

FADE IN:

<u>TITLE CARD</u>: *DOC DYNAMO* followed by minimal CREDITS, then–

<u>TITLE CARD</u>: *"CHAPTER TWO: BLAZING DOOM!"*

(<u>NOTE</u>: *CHAPTER OPENS WITH A REPRISE OF THE MOVIETOWN NEWSREEL, AND EDITED FOOTAGE FROM THE PREVIOUS CHAPTER'S CLIFFHANGER, ENDING WITH...*)

<u>EXT. WHITE LIGHTNING - CLOSE ON DOC - NIGHT</u>
Doc's eyes are wide behind his goggles–almost paralyzed by indecision. Then, teeth gritted, he makes his decision!

DASHBOARD
Doc's hand flicks a toggle switch marked AUTOMATIC DRIVER, then–

CHOICE #1: DOC STAYS TO SAVE RICKY

<u>EXT. THE MOUNTAIN ROAD</u>
as White Lightning ROARS BY toward Dead Man's Curve, Doc climbs over the front seat, onto the trunk of the two-seater.

CHOICE #2: DOC JUMPS

<u>EXT. THE ROAD</u>
Doc leaps from driver's seat into the darkness as White Lightning zooms along. He hits the ground, and springs back instantly, landing on the trunk of the two-seater.

(*FOOTAGE FROM THE TWO "CHOICES" COMBINES HERE.*)

WHITE LIGHTNING - FRONT SEAT
ROBOT HANDS, on the ends of thin metal robot "arms," complete with elbow joints, jut out from a secret compartment on the driver's seat and take the wheel, holding it steady.

Wind tears at Doc as he clings to the trunk, facing backward so that he works the key upside down. The latch is jammed.

INT. TRUNK

                    RICKY
     Sorry, Doc! I guess I broke the latch when I got in!

EXT. MOUNTAIN ROAD - WHITE LIGHTNING
Doc looks over his shoulder, apprehensively.

DOC'S POV - DEAD MAN'S CURVE
Caught in headlights, a second road sign reading DEAD MAN'S CURVE coming up fast.

Doc reaches to his belt, still clinging upside down onto the trunk.

                    RICKY (O.S.)
     Doc? Hey, Doc? Are you mad at me?

DOC'S BELT
Doc pulls a weird-looking device from his belt–like a 1940s version of a laser gun, or something equally Buck-Rogersy.

Robot hands frantically guide the car. One of them flicks ash off a cigarette between its "fingers."

Doc brings device to the latch, and presses a button on the side of device, which HUMS ELECTRONICALLY, LOUDER, LOUDER, until–

DEVICE

–it suddenly a spring-loaded screwdriver bit snaps out. Using the bit, Doc quickly snaps the latch. Immediately the trunk hood flings upward, smashing Doc off the car.

EXT. ROADSIDE – NIGHT

Doc lands at the side of the road. Rolls over once, is up on his feet in an instant–in time for the leaping Ricky to land in his arms. Setting him down, Doc looks up to see:

EXT. MOUNTAIN ROAD

White Lightning crashes through the guard rail, in a long, almost graceful arc out into the night–

EXT. ROADSIDE LAKE

–to splash down noisily in a lake, not far below the level of the road itself.

EXT. ROADSIDE

> RICKY
>
> Guess that means the bad guys'll get away, huh, Doc?

Doc and Ricky look down the road toward the SOUND OF ENGINES.

THEIR POV - THUNDER'S TRUCK AND THUNDER-WAGON

ROAR into the darkness, around a curve, and are gone.

> DOC
>
> I guess that's what it means, all right.

WIPE TO:

EXT. DESERT HIDEOUT - NIGHT

A small, lonely shack in the middle of nowhere. The Thunder's truck and the Thunderwagon bump along the dirt road approaching it.

Shortie jumps from the truck, goes to the shack and works an old cistern pump in front of it. The entire front of the shack tilts upward like a garage door opener to admit the truck.

The Thunderwagon swings around the shack to park at the rear.

INT. SECRET LABORATORY - NIGHT

The truck RUMBLES into a huge lab, many times larger than the shack seems from outside.

As The Thunder enters on foot, the wall swings shut.

The lab is on two levels: the main floor, surrounded by a cat-walk balcony about 15 feet up. Support pillars and ladders connect the balcony to the floor below. At one end of the room, a LARGE TURBINE GENERATOR WHIRS to life at The Thunder's touch–and a moment later, lights flicker on. The windowless chamber is filled to the brim with generators, lab equipment and a Tele-Visor.

The Thunder leaves Shortie and Longjohn to unload the engine as he activates the Tele-Visor.

Gams settles herself on a desk, checks a run in her stocking as she listens to The Thunder. Flickering test-patterns zip across the Tele-Visor screen, the image finally settling into that of Adolf Hitler.

> THUNDER
> Mein Fuhrer... I have captured the Keppler Rocket-plane Engine, as you commanded.

HITLER
(in Japanese)
What did you say? I can't understand you.

THUNDER
Just a moment, Mein Fuhrer. Something seems to be
wrong with the Techno-Magnetic Voice Translator.

HITLER
(in Russian)
Then fix it, you idiot, or–
(suddenly, in English)
–I will have you shot!
(recognizes change)
Ach, that's better. You say you have the engine?
What about the American agent, Doc Dynamite?

THUNDER
Dynamo, Mein Fuhrer. He's dead.

HITLER
See that he stays that way! With the Keppler Rocketplane engine in our hands, we will be invincible!

THUNDER
Would you care for a demonstration of the engine's
power, Mein Fuhrer?

HITLER
(rubs his hands)
Ach, jawhol!

The Thunder strides purposefully to the center of the chamber,
where Shortie and Longjohn have set the engine prototype on
a tripod.

Gams watches from the side, striking a match on her stocking and lighting a cigarette. With a flourish, The Thunder presses a large red button on the side of the engine.

The prototype gives a pathetic WHEEZE; SMOKE COUGHS from its rear end.

Gams coughs smoke from her cigarette in surprise.

The Thunder gapes at the prototype, then angrily pounds it with his fist. Gams looks over his shoulder, taps a fuel gauge that reads EMPTY.

                    GAMS
          Bad news, Thundy. You're out of gas. I told you we
          should've stopped at that Texaco station.

The Thunder whirls angrily on Shortie and Longjohn, slapping them across the faces with one sweep of his hand, *à la* Three Stooges.

                    THUNDER
          Scheiskopfs!
               (to Hitler)
          It's nothing, Mein Fuhrer. The Rocketplane runs on a
          special liquid fuel. I can easily obtain the fuel
          through my connection with the Icarus Aircraft Com-
          pany.

                    HITLER
          The fools still do not suspect that you are one of
          them?

                    THUNDER
          On the contrary, Mein Fuhrer. In their eyes, the man
          beneath this mask is a loyal patriot. If only they knew
          I am the viper in their midst!

49

He laughs maniacally, and Hitler joins him. Shortie and Longjohn exchange a look and laugh along, nervously. Gams raises her eyes to heaven as MAD LAUGHTER ECHOES in the chamber.

WIPE TO:

<u>EXT. EMPIRE STATE BUILDING - MORNING</u>
Still wet and dripping, White Lightning pulls up in front of the building, stops. Passers-by pass by, without pause. Ricky opens the passenger-side door–and several gallons of water (not to mention a few fish) cascade out onto the sidewalk.

                    RICKY
          Hey, Doc, maybe we can do this again sometime.
          Whaddaya say?

                    DOC
          I'll give it some thought. Give my regards to your
          charming sister, Nurse Wallace, and her generous
          employer, Dr. Fred Franklin, the pediatrician.

                    RICKY
               (rolling his eyes knowingly)
          Oh, I sure will, Doc. Hey, why don't you come in?
          I'm sure Dr. Fred'd love to meet you.

                    DOC
          Er, uh–some other time, son.

Ricky closes the door, and Doc drives off.

WIPE TO:

INT. DR. FRED'S OFFICE DOOR - MORNING
CLOSE on the sign reading: *DR. FRED FRANKLIN, PEDIA-TRICIAN.*

INT. DR. FRED'S OFFICE - MORNING
Ricky enters–is astonished to see Dr. Fred, wincing as Nurse Nancy applies iodine to some minor cuts. Dr. Fred's white smock is rumpled, his Doc Dynamo jacket reversed.

NANCY

Oh, hi, Ricky.

DR. FRED

How was the double feature, son?

RICKY

Boy, you sure got up here fast!

DR. FRED

Why, er, what do you mean, Ricky? I've been here all morning. Haven't I, Nurse Wallace?

NANCY

Right in this very chair.

RICKY

Oh yeah? How'd he get them bruises?

DR. FRED

Well, I, er...

NANCY

He fell off the chair. You sure ask a lot of questions, little brother.

                          DR. FRED
          Er, Nurse Wallace... don't you inkthay we should get
          idray of the idkay, so we can alktay?

Nurse Nancy, used to English, has trouble following this.

                          RICKY
          Oh, no. You don't get rid of me that easy. I'm not
          moving.

Dr. Fred and Nurse Nancy look awkwardly at each other; Dr.
Fred starts to whistle and rearrange some sterilization equipment. Ricky waits them out. Abruptly, Ace Burlington pops
his head in the door, all smiles and (so he believes) boyish
charm.

                          ACE
          Hi there, crime-stoppers! Am I interrupting anything
          personal, I hope, I hope?

                          DR. FRED
          Oh, hello, Police Inspector Burlington.

                          ACE
          "Ace," remember?

                          DR. FRED
          Ace.

Ace slaps Dr. Fred heartily on the back, causing him to drop a
tray of sterilized instruments. As Dr. Fred stoops to pick it all
up, Nurse Nancy looks at him with frustrated disappointment.

                          NANCY
                    (slight edge to voice)
          What do you want this time... Ace?

                            52

ACE

Same thing I always want, passion flower. A date
with my favorite Florence Nightingale.

NANCY

Gee, Ace... you really know how to talk to a girl.

ACE
(sotto voce)
I'm still hot on the trail of that spy they call The
Thunder. I'll bet he's shakin' in his jackboots right
about now!
(grins)
What've I gotta do to make the Hit parade with you?
Bring in Dillinger?

Nancy and Dr. Fred exchange glances, look at Ricky.

NANCY

Well, actually... my brother Ricky's a big fan of
yours.

RICKY

Huh? Hey, waitamminit, sis–

NANCY

Maybe you could take him along while you're track-
ing down spies and saboteurs–

RICKY

Oh no you don't!

NANCY

–you know, to show him what real police work is
like–not that silly Doc Dynamo stuff he's always
going on about. Please?

She bats her eyelashes.

>   ACE
>   (disdainfully)
>   "Doc Dynamo!"
>   (patting Ricky on head as he leads
>   him out the door)
>   No offense, kiddo, but that masked buttinski can't
>   hold a candle to a real cop like Dick Tracy–or to
>   some others I could tell you about. If I wasn't so
>   modest...

Ricky glares and Ace gives Nancy a wink as she shuts
the door behind him and Ricky. She leans against it, sighing.

>   DR. FRED
>   Doesn't your kid brother have any closer relatives he
>   could live with?

>   NANCY
>   You were saying, about the engine prototype?

>   DR. FRED
>   If The Thunder manages to smuggle it out of the
>   country, the Nazis could soon be mass-producing
>   propellor-less Rocketplanes and win the war.

>   NANCY
>   They'll want to test it first. What about fuel?

>   DR. FRED
>   (snaps his fingers)
>   That's right. Chief Engineer Palmer told me the
>   Rocketplane works on a special liquid fuel... Let's
>   check the Electro-Robot Directory.

He goes to an old-fashioned rolltop desk, pulls up the lid to reveal an odd combination of Underwood typewriter and the 1940 New York Yellow Pages, connected with wires and metal struts. Dr. Fred quickly runs his fingers over the typewriter keys. The directory snaps open, pulled by the struts, and pages flutter right to left–falling open near the center. A metal pointer runs down a column of names, stops at one.

The POINTER underlines a listing that reads: *LIQUID PLUMMET FUEL COMPANY.*

Dr. Fred turns from the directory, grinning.

                    DR. FRED
        This is a job for–

Dr. Fred throws off his smock, revealing that he is still wearing his Doc Dynamo outfit underneath it. He retrieves his helmet from a wastebasket, puts it on, lowers the goggles into place.

                    DOC
              (an octave lower)
        Doc Dynamo!

NANCY'S EYES are glaze, with a dual image of Doc Dynamo. Appropriate MUSIC.

Doc starts toward the front door. Nancy shakes off her daze.

                    NANCY
        Wait, Doc. You may need help. This time, I'm coming with you.

They stride to the outer office door, pull it open.

                    WIPE TO:

55

EXT. ICARUS AIRCRAFT BUILDING - DAY

INT. ICARUS BOARDROOM - DAY
Dr. Harry Lanton is seated at head of conference table.
PHONE RINGS. He picks it up, has a staccato conversation
with person on other end.

> ### LANTON
> Dr. Lanton, President of Icarus Aircraft here. Oh–
> hello, Doc Dynamo. I see, Doc Dynamo. Thank you,
> Doc Dynamo.
> > (hangs up)
>
> That was Doc Dynamo.

BOARDROOM
seated around table as before are Keppler, Chislewit, Palmer
and (on folding chair) Hooper. All wear identical suits, different from those in Chapter One. Behind them, two WORK-
MEN finish installing a new plate glass window.

> ### LANTON
> He's at the Liquid Plummet Company. They just got
> a call ordering every gallon of liquid fuel in its stock.
> Doc Dynamo figures that call must have come from
> The Thunder. He plans to trap The Thunder and his
> men by having his female assistant–we'll call her
> "Miss X"–pose as a male truck driver to lure The
> Thunder out of hiding, and that's when Doc Dynamo
> will spring his foolproof trap!

> ### CHISLEWIT
> He said all that just then?

> ### LANTON
> Doc Dynamo's not a man to mince words, Chislewit.
> Keppler–do you think it'll work?

KEPPLER

Ja, it might. Mein Keppler Rocketplane is good, but it
will not run on empty, nein?

PALMER

(pounding table with fist)
Then we've got them, by thunder–
(realizing what he's said)
–you should excuse the expression.

CHISLEWIT

(figuring with an adding machine)
All I know is, losing that prototype has cost us another $12 million on top of the original $20
million. At this rate, Icarus Aircraft can keep operat-
ing another–
(quits)
–37 hours and 14 minutes.

Lanton turns to Hooper, who's scribbling all that down.

LANTON

Don't write that down, Hooper. Do you want our
stockholders on our necks when they read the minutes?

HOOPER

No, sir, Mr. Lanton, sir.

Hooper hurriedly starts to erase the entry from his notebook.

LANTON

And remember, secrecy is essential. The knowledge
that Doc Dynamo is laying a trap for The Thunder
must not leave this room, or Dynamo could be in
deadly danger!

The other boardmen murmur their assent, one by one. Yet each looks shifty-eyed, suspicious. Which of them is secretly The Thunder?

WIPE TO:

<u>EXT. CITY STREET - DAY</u>
Ace Burlington's car (with NYPD markings) rolls along. Ace, chomping on an apple, is trying to impress a bored Ricky.

ACE

> See, little chum? Real police work is a lot more ex-
> citing than all that Doc Dynamo stuff, isn't it?

RICKY

> (starts awake)
> Huh? What? Sure.

He goes back to a doze. Suddenly there is a LOUD, STATICKY SQUAWKING from Ace's two-way wrist walkie-talkie:

WALKIE-TALKIE

> Calling Inspector Burlington. Calling Inspector Bur-
> lington.

Ace bangs his forehead with the walkie-talkie, trying to get it to his ear while still driving the car.

The car swerves out of control; Ricky grabs the wheel; Ace fumbles with the walkie-talkie's switches.

ACE

> Ace here. What's up?

> WALKIE-TALKIE
> Just got a tip-off that Doc Dynamo's car's been seen following a liquid fuel truck over on Republic Avenue. May have something to do with the theft yesterday at Icarus Aircraft.

> ACE
> It sure might! I'm gonna check it out. Over and out.
>> (switches off, gets the wheel back
>> from Ricky)
> OK, hang onto your bubblegum, kid–'cause here we go!

Ace reaches down to turn on SIREN.

Ace's car, SIREN SCREECHING, peels out.

> RICKY (V.O.)
> All right!

CUT TO:

EXT. LONG ISLAND BACK ROAD - DAY
A Liquid Plummet fuel truck barrels along. Motto on side: "If it's wet, it's LIQUID."

TRUCK CAB
Nurse Nancy, disguised as a male truck driver, complete with five o'clock shadow and singing a song of the open road in as deep a voice as she can manage. She chomps on a cigar, coughs, chokes.

The White Lightning races along some distance behind.

Doc drives, jaw jutting.

Nurse Nancy glances down at fuel gauge. It's nearly empty. She looks up.

NANCY'S POV - GAS STATION SIGN - reading: *SPECIAL TODAY FOR LIQUID FUEL TRUCKS.*

EXT. GAS STATION - DAY
The liquid fuel truck pulls up to the pumps. Disguised Nancy gets out as Shortie, disguised as attendant, approaches.

> NANCY
> Fill 'er up. Uh, do you have a clean restroom?

Shortie indicates the side of the station.

EXT. GAS STATION RESTROOMS - DAY
Nancy stops equidistant between the doors marked *MEN* and *WOMEN*. Stands scratching her head; can't decide which to use.

INT. MEN'S RESTROOM - DAY
Longjohn waits near door, tire iron in hand.

INT. WOMEN'S RESTROOM - DAY
Gams Catling waits, gun in hand, adjusting her silk stockings.

EXT. GAS STATION RESTROOMS

> NANCY (shrugs)
> Oh, the hell with it.

She starts to walk away, trips over Shortie, who is on his hands and knees directly behind her. As she struggles with him, Gams and Longjohn rush from the rest-rooms and join in, when suddenly–

The White Lightning SCREECHES onto scene. Doc Dynamo leaps out, and into fray.

THE FIGHT
A knock-down, drag-out, Republic-Serials-style fight, with flailing fists in slightly speeded-up footage. Longjohn swings his tire iron, but Doc leaps impossibly high, over the blow— and comes down with both feet in Longjohn's face. He somersaults over the falling Longjohn, as Gams FIRES at him.

A STRAY BULLET hits the nearest gasoline pump, and it ERUPTS INTO FLAME.

Doc and Longjohn struggle, inches from the burning pump. Doc gets a fist loose and slugs Longjohn first, then Shortie. Both go tumbling backward, Longjohn slamming into Gams and knocking her down so that her gun goes flying.

Nancy is still on the ground, confused.

Longjohn rolls an oil barrel at Doc, who leaps onto it like a lumberjack on log. Doc rides the rolling barrel into Shortie, then grabs him up and swings Shortie like a battering ram into Longjohn's stomach.

Longjohn hops backward, grabbing his gut. Doc raises his fist for a crushing blow to Longjohn's jaw, when–

–Gams gets her gun to Nancy's temple.

> GAMS
> Hold it, Dynamo, or I'll shoot this truck driver!

> NANCY
> (in own voice)
> Call her bluff, Doc. I'm not important. You're all that matters.

Gams reacts to fact that Nancy is a woman in disguise. Doc lowers his fist, helplessly.

> GAMS
> Oh, so you're sweet on him, too, are you? That makes you the perfect hostage–to make sure he doesn't interfere again.
> (to Doc)
> So long, handsome. Let's go, boys.

She and Longjohn rush Nancy to the fuel truck. Shortie follows. Obviously frustrated, Doc watches the truck pull away–then puts fingers to his lips and whistles.

The White Lightning ROARS TO LIFE, turning in a sharp circle to allow Doc to leap onto its running board.

Robot hands turn the steering wheel, as White Lightning tears off in hot pursuit of the fuel truck.

TRAVELING SHOT
DOC riding White Lightning's running board as the car pulls up behind the truck. Doc leaps from the running board to the fuel truck's rear access ladder.

TRUCK CAB
Gams looks at her side mirror, sees White Lightning pulling up alongside on the left. She sneers, yanks the wheel to the left.

The White Lightning, sideswiped by the fuel truck, careens off the road into a ditch.

TRUCK'S ROOF
Doc, on the fuel truck's roof, looks back with a pang at his faithful car, spinning its wheels half-upside down.

ROAD MAP OF LONG ISLAND

A MOVING LINE (*à la Raiders of Lost Ark* sub sequence) traces a meandering path all over it, finally doubling back to a point near where it started.

INT. THUNDER'S SECRET LAB - DAY

The truck RUMBLES IN, door closing behind it. Doc is on the truck's roof, crouched and ready for action. The Thunder enters through a secret door from another part of the lab.

>   GAMS
>   We got the fuel, Thundy–and Doc Dynamo's own
>   personal gal friend.

>   THUNDER
>   Tie her up over there.

Thunder indicates a support pillar ten feet from the tripod-mounted engine prototype. Nancy struggles in Shortie's grip.

>   NANCY
>   (defiantly)
>   Doc Dynamo will steal your thunder yet, Thunder.

>   THUNDER
>   Oh yes–and be sure to gag her.

Shortie and Gams tie Nancy to the pole, as Longjohn starts pumping liquid fuel into gas tank of the engine prototype.

>   WIPE TO:

EXT. ROADSIDE DITCH

Ace's car SCREECHES to a halt. Ace hops out and goes to White Lightning, followed by Ricky.

                         RICKY
          This is Doc's car, all right. He took me for a ride in it
          just this morning.

                         ACE
          So where is he?

                         RICKY
                    (pointing)
          Look!

Ricky runs over to a trail of liquid fuel on the road.

                         ACE
          Liquid fuel... Better not step in it, kid. That stuff's
          messy.

                         RICKY
          Don't you see? Doc Dynamo must've cut a hole in
          the tank of the fuel truck, figuring that way we could
          follow it.

                         ACE
                    (light slowly dawning)
          Doc Dynamo must've cut a hole in the tank of the
          fuel truck, figuring that way we could follow it. Let's
          go!

They both pile into Ace's car, and he peels out onto road.

                                             WIPE TO:

INT. SECRET LAB
Nancy is tied and gagged to the support pillar, the engine exhaust pointed right at her. Longjohn finishes fueling up the
prototype.

                    LONGJOHN
All gassed up, Boss.

                    THUNDER
You, Miss X, will be the first American victim of Der
Fuhrer's new Rocketplane.
               (as she writhes, mumbles)
No, it's too late to apologize.

The Thunder is about to press the start button, hand poised,
when–

Doc Dynamo leaps onto him from the roof of the truck, somersaulting in mid-air. The Thunder goes down, Doc wrestling
with him. Shortie and Longjohn rush to Thunder's rescue, and
soon Doc is fighting with them, another slugfest. The Thunder
works himself free...

The Thunder presses the start button.

The engine prototype FIRES UP; we can see and hear its JET
EXHAUST growing stronger, stronger... fire pouring out of
engine.

Nancy in its path–the fire coming closer, closer as she struggles...

                                        ZIP WIPE TO:

EXT. DESERT HIDEOUT/SHACK
Ace's car SCREECHES to a halt, dust flying. Ricky is thrown
to the floor by the sharp stop.

                    RICKY
        Nice brakes.

ACE
The trail ends here. They must be inside that shack.
I've got 'em now! You stay here, kid.

He gets out of car. Naturally, so does Ricky.

Ace has no luck with the (painted-on) shack door–it doesn't
even have a real doorknob. He keeps trying–really confused.

Ricky looks over the cistern, suspiciously. He works the
pump, tin cup in hand. No water comes out.

Suddenly, the entire front of the shack tilts upward, clipping
Ace's chin. Ace staggers back, amazed. Ricky runs to him.

RICKY
Wow! A secret door! How'd you find it?

ACE
(rubs his chin)
Years of special police training. You stay here.

He goes inside. Ricky follows as if he hadn't spoken.

INT. SECRET LAB
Ace and Ricky find themselves inside the lab, where Doc's
round-housing it out with Shortie and Longjohn as Gams
looks on, excited. The secret DOOR RUMBLES SHUT behind them.

The Thunder sees them, reacts–and pulls a switch on the wall.

A section of ceiling SLAMS DOWN right in front of Ace and
Ricky, trapping them between it and the secret door. They beat
their fists in vain against both walls.

                              ACE
              Well, at least we're safe here.

Abruptly, with an ominous RUMBLING, the ceiling overhead–laced with stalactite-like spikes–starts to descend toward
them. Ricky grimaces at Ace.

                            RICKY
              You had to say that, right?

Nurse Nancy struggles to no avail as the fiery exhaust inches
closer and closer.

Doc uppercuts Shortie, which drives the smaller man's head
into Longjohn's chin. Both men go down, and Doc grins,
cracking his knuckles, until Gams Catling smashes a crowbar
over his head. He sinks slowly to the floor, Gams standing
over him.

                           THUNDER
                   (as Rocketplane overheats)
              Gams! The controls are jammed... It's going to ex-
              plode!

He runs for a rear exit. Shortie and Longjohn follow groggily.
Gams hesitates, looking back at Doc with an almost wistful
expression. She blows him a kiss, runs out, as Doc staggers to
his feet, holding his head. He looks anxiously around:

DOC'S POV - FRONT OF SHACK
Sinister RUMBLING and GRINDING SOUNDS come from
the sealed wall, along with muffled but distinct cries of "Help,
Doc!"

Doc jerks his head back the other way–

                              67

DOC'S POV - ENGINE AND NANCY
The FIERY EXHAUST draws closer to Nancy, as she mumbles through what's left of her gag.

> NANCY
> Help, Doc! Help!

Doc looks both ways–

> DOC
> I can't save you both. There's no time!

He looks helplessly at the CAMERA.

> NARRATOR (O.S.)
> The choice is yours! Should Doc save little Ricky and
> Inspector Ace–

Ricky and Ace in dire straits.

SUPERED TITLE: *CHOICE #1: SAVE RICKY AND IN-SPECTOR ACE?*

> NARRATOR (O.S.) (cont'd)
> –or should he rescue Nurse Nancy from a fiery
> doom?

Nancy struggling as smoke rises.

SUPERED TITLE: *CHOICE #2: SAVE NURSE NANCY?*

CLOSE - FLAMING ENGINE

SUPERED TITLE: "*Don't miss CHAPTER THREE: BLASTS
OF PERIL!*"

                    NARRATOR (O.S.) (cont'd)
To learn which answer you choose, keep watching
this channel for the next pulse-pounding episode of
"Doc Dynamo!"

                              FADE OUT.

FADE IN:

TITLE CARD: "*DOC DYNAMO–America's Ace Spy-Swatter.*" Minimal credits, triumphant MUSIC, followed by (on a down note):

TITLE CARD: "*CHAPTER THREE: BLAST OF DOOM!*"

WIPE TO:

(NOTE: *CHAPTER OPENS WITH A REPRISE OF THE MOVIETOWN NEWSREEL, AND EDITED FOOTAGE FROM THE PREVIOUS CHAPTER'S CLIFFHANGER, END-ING WITH...*)

INT. SECRET LAB
Doc makes his decision–

WIDER
Nancy coughing as Doc tries to get to her, but can't. The smoke is too thick and black.

THE SEALED WALL
The muffled BANGING and YELLING is fainter now.

INT. THE SEALED WALL
Ace and Ricky are squeezed up close to the spikes as the ceiling lowers.

INT. SECRET LAB – CLOSE
Doc pulls open the collar of his flight suit–lifts out a white gas mask, fits it over his face. He pushes a switch on the side of his flight goggles, and a red film drops down under the glass.

DOC'S POV - INFRA-RED LENS VIEW
The prototype is visible through the smoke as a *glowing red shape*.

Nancy coughing, passes out, her clothes smoldering.

Doc looks around, and rips an eight-foot length of piping from the wall of the shack. Holding it like a pole-vaulter, he runs toward the smoke, jams it into the floor and swings *over* the smoke cloud.

Doc's feet come down, slams into the prototype, spinning it around.

CHOICE #1: SAVE NANCY

The Exhaust shoots inches past Nancy's slumped figure as the engine spins, severing the pillar above her head. The engine spins on–

INT. THE SEALED WALL
Ace and Ricky almost touching spikes, both trying in vain to hold back the wall.

INT. SECRET LAB
The prototype's continuing spin sends the yards-long flame from the exhaust ROARING across the room, toward the sealed wall.

THE SEALED WALL
is cut through near the ceiling by the engine's exhaust, as if by a blowtorch. A SIZZLING POP.

The wall falls outward with a CRASH, spilling Ace and Ricky roughly to the floor of the lab.

CHOICE #2: SAVE RICKY AND ACE

INT. THE SEALED WALL
Ace and Ricky almost touching spikes, both trying in vain to hold back the wall.

INT. SECRET LAB
The prototype's continuing spin sends the yards-long flame from the exhaust ROARING across the room, toward the sealed wall.

THE SEALED WALL
is cut through near the ceiling by the engine's exhaust, as if by a blowtorch. A SIZZLING POP.

The wall falls outward with a CRASH, spilling Ace and Ricky roughly to the floor of the lab.

The exhaust shoots inches past Nancy's slumped figure as the engine continues to spin, severing the pillar above her head.

(*FOOTAGE FROM THE TWO CHOICES COMBINES HERE.*)

THE PROTOTYPE
Doc's hand reaches INTO FRAME, to push a button marked OFF.

The exhaust shuts OFF with a SPUTTER and HISS.

Doc lifts Nancy from the pillar, carries her out through the smoke. Nancy is still gagged, hands tied... just waking up. Groggy, she looks around at–

NANCY'S POV
Ace and Ricky up on the raised floor-section. Ricky waves enthusiastically at her. Ace is in a daze.

> RICKY
> Hi, sis! Some fun, huh?

EXT. DESERT SHACK - DAY

Doc and company stumble coughing from the fake shack front into the sunlight, smoke pouring out behind them. Doc sets her down a bit roughly in the clear, as Ricky lets go of Ace–who goes down like a rock.

Doc nods to Ricky and both of them rush back into the shack front, to return seconds later, pushing the engine prototype before them on its wheeled tripod. Ace is still out, as Doc and Ricky go to Nancy. She mumbles through her gag, struggling to get loose. Doc, standing above her, looks meaningfully at Ricky.

> DOC
> I'm afraid Nurse Wallace is right, Ricky. The
> Thunder and his mob have made their getaway...
> and left us without a clue.

> RICKY
> Hey, no sweat, Doc. At least you managed to save the
> rocket engine. Things're going great. Right, sis?

At last, Nancy manages to yank a hand free from her bindings and quickly tears her gag off, gasping and choking for air.

WIPE TO:

EXT. DESERT ROADWAY - DAY

The Thunderwagon ROARS along the dusty road, somewhere on the Long Island desert.

THUNDERWAGON

The Thunder at the wheel, Shortie and Longjohn together in back, Gams gazing wistfully out the passenger window, murmuring softly to herself...

GAMS
He sure was good-looking...

THUNDER
What was that, Gams?

GAMS
Hm? Oh, nothing. Nothing at all.

THUNDER
Shortie, Longjohn... Listen to me. If that fool Inspector was able to trail us, others might follow. So
after I return to Icarus Aircraft, I want you to move
the hideout.

SHORTIE
Aw, boss... do we have to?

LONGJOHN
I almost got a hernia the last time.

The Thunder gives them a cold look.

THUNDER
Wear a truss.

WIPE TO:

EXT. DESERT ROADWAY - DUSK
Ace Burlington's patrol car bumps along the dusty road toward the spot where we last saw The Thunder's hide-out.
Newspaper Reporters and Photographers jam the car, listening
skeptically.

ACE
(in mid-sentence)
–you heard me, boys. I took on the whole nest of
spies single-handed. Make sure you get the name
right for your papers. Ace Burlington. Inspector Ace
Burlington of the Bigtown... police...

His voice trails off.

Ahead, standing in the middle of nowhere, all alone, is the
cistern pump. There's no sign of the shack. Burlington's car
trundles slowly to a stop, as his voice trails off.

Ace looks at the hostile newsmen with desperation.

ACE
Maybe I took a wrong turn?

DISSOLVE TO:

EXT. ICARUS AIRCRAFT BUILDING - NIGHT

INT. ICARUS AIRCRAFT BOARDROOM – NIGHT
Lanton casts a slow, lingering gaze around the board table.

LANTON
Gentlemen... I have an important announcement to
make. The Rocketplane engine prototype has been
rescued from The Thunder–and is once more safe
under guard at our factory, at this very moment.

The board members and Hooper applaud. Palmer bangs a fist
on the table with a loud "By Godfrey!" All four Board members and Hooper are now clad in a third type of identical suit.
Lanton silences them all with a curt gesture.

                    LANTON (cont'd)
        I'm afraid there's more. Gentlemen... much as it
        pains me to say it, I must tell you that I have come to
        the conclusion that one of us in this room... is a trair.

REACTION SHOTS - PALMER, KEPPLER, CHISLEWIT
glance shifty-eyed from one to another.

                    LANTON (O.S.)
        Chief Engineer Palmer... Chief Designer Keppler...
        Chief Accountant Chislewit... one of you men has
        betrayed his country, and what's more, this company.
                    (folding his arms)
        And, what's more, we're not leaving this room until I
        find out who.

                    HOOPER
        Uh... that's "whom," Mr. Lanton.

                    LANTON
        Shut up, Hooper.

A long, drawn-out beat, broken only by the skittering of
Hooper's pencil on his notepad. Keppler attempts to light a
cigarette in a long holder, but his hand's too shaky. Chislewit
pours himself a glass of water, spilling some as he drinks.
Palmer nervously runs a finger around his collar; it has an
obvious dark ring.

                    LANTON (cont'd)
                    (impatiently)
        Well? I'm waiting.
                    (as Keppler raises hand)
        Yes, Herr Doctor Keppler?

KEPPLER
(very, very softly)
Vot about you?

LANTON
Speak up. I'm sure we'd all like to hear what you
have to say.

KEPPLER
Vot iff it's you, Herr Lanton?

An awkward pause. Lanton nonplussed.

LANTON
Well, I... It could be me, of course... but it isn't... I
mean... I'm pretty certain about that... really... after
all, I'm the President of this company...

CHISLEWIT
(takes out his adding machine)
A company that's already $23 million in the red be-
cause of this ill-advised Rocketplane experiment. By
my calculations, we're losing an additional $.7 mil-
lion every hour. At this rate...
(looks at watch)
Only 23 hours and 38 minutes to go before total
bankruptcy and ruin.

PALMER
(bangs his fist)
By Heaven, it makes sense! Lanton must be the traitor!

LANTON
(desperately)
What about Keppler? He's even a German, for God's
sake!

PALMER
(bangs his fist)
By Heaven, it makes sense! Keppler must be the
traitor!

KEPPLER
I am not German! I am Sviss! Besides, vot about
Chislevit? All dot money he's always talking about
us losing... maybe he embezzled it himself.

PALMER
(bangs his fist)
By Heaven, it makes sense! Chislewit must be the
traitor!

CHISLEWIT
What about Palmer? His engineering department is
always running on overtime... trying to drive us to
bankruptcy!

PALMER
(bangs his fist)
By Heaven, it makes sense! I must be the traitor!
(takes)
Wait a minute...

In an uproar, the board members shout at each other, AD
LIBBING accusations and threats. Suddenly, Doc Dynamo
comes swinging in through the window again, SHATTERING
THE GLASS a second time. He walks to the table, GLASS
CRUNCHING under his feet as before.

DOC
Gentlemen... forgive me, but I have some bad news
for you–something which I know will shock and re-
volt you, even as it shocked and revolted me.

(dramatic beat)
I have studied this case, and one thing seems clear,
after this last ambush. Impossible as I know you will
find it to believe—one of you men is a traitor.

Utter silence. Doc waits expectantly. They stare at him.

                    DOC (cont'd)
                (clears his throat)
          Yes. Well. Think about it.

He strides toward the door. Lanton rises hurriedly.

                    LANTON
          Doc Dynamo—wait.

Doc turns.

                    LANTON (cont'd)
          In view of the urgency of the situation, I think we've
          no choice but to schedule that delayed final test as
          soon as possible—tomorrow morning at ten o'clock.
          Do you agree, gentlemen?
                (as board members all mumble assent)
          Will you be on hand to protect the engine prototype
          from The Thunder, this one last time?

Behind his goggles, Doc cocks an eyebrow... and smiles.

                                        WIPE TO:

EXT. CITY STREET - NIGHT
Office buildings loom in the darkness as the BELL-CHIMES
ECHO O.S. Between two towering Art Deco office buildings,
in a vacant lot, sits The Thunder's shack hideout, looking
lonely and out of place. A shadowy figure enters the shack
furtively.

INT. THUNDER'S SECRET LAB - NIGHT
As lights come on, the shadowy figure is revealed to be The Thunder. Quickly he moves to the Tele-Visor on one wall, activates it. Hitler appears on the screen.

> ### THUNDER
> Mein Fuhrer. I have good news, and bad news. The bad news is, we've lost the Rocketplane engine prototype. The good news is, I have a plan...

> WIPE TO:

INT. DOOR TO DR. FRED'S OFFICE - DAY
Nancy's VOICE ON SOUND, from inside.

> ### NANCY (O.S.)
> No, I'm sorry, Inspector Burlington...

> ### ACE (O.S.)
> Ace.

INT. DR. FRED'S OFFICE - DAY
Nancy is trying to look busy as she tidies up the office. But Ace Burlington won't be put off. The wall clock reads 9:00.

> ### NANCY
> Ace. But I really don't know anything more about Doc Dynamo than you do. I just happened to be passing by...

> ### ACE
> The Thunder's secret hideout? Dressed as a male truck driver?

> ### NANCY
> (a weak smile)
> Call it a whim.

ACE

Being in cahoots, that's what Dick Tracy would call it–and that's what Ace Burlington calls it, too!

NANCY

(her back up)

Oh, really?

(switching to coy mode)

And here I thought you were still hanging around because you wanted a date with me.

ACE

(discombobulated)

I was–I mean, I am! After all, there's another big Battle of the Bands tomorrow night. But I'm still a police officer–and to me, any guy who runs around hiding behind a mask–

(before Nancy can correct him)

–or goggles–is a crook!

NANCY

Even if he saved your life?

ACE

That could have been an accident. There was so much smoke, I couldn't see a thing. For all I know, Doc Dynamo's working hand in glove with The Thunder. So when they run that secret field test on the Rocketplane prototype this morning, Ace Burlington's gonna be on hand to stop any wise stuff. Nobody makes a fool out of me without I know about it.

He leaves angrily. Nancy stares after him a moment, then opens the door marked *PRIVATE*. She gives a scream when she finds Ricky grinning at her on the other side.

                              RICKY
Hi, sis.

                              NANCY
Ricky!

                              RICKY
Somebody better warn Doc Dynamo about Inspector
Ace. I guess we're elected.

                              NANCY
                      (with a resigned sigh)
I guess you're right.

                              RICKY
                      (as they head out)
So where's Dr. Fred?

                              NANCY
On a house call.

Ricky rolls his eyes.

                                        CROSS WIPE TO:

EXT. NEW JERSEY AERODROME – DAY
A collection of hangars and runways in a wooded section of
New Jersey. Small single-engine races lift into the sky, land.

ANGLE - FRONT GATE
Dr. Fred, in pediatrician's smock, forehead reflector band, and
carrying a black doctor's bag, shows his identification to the
elderly watchman, POP.

                              DR. FRED
Medical emergency. One of the engineers is ill with
an advanced case of Contagiousitus.

                              POP
Is that bad?

                              DR. FRED
It isn't good.

Pop swallows heavily and waves him through the gate.

EXT. FACTORY BUILDING – DAY
A Coca-Cola wall clock reads: 9:50 as Dr. Fred approaches a
public phone booth with glass walls and door. He glances
about furtively to see if he's observed, then ducks into the
booth and changes to Doc Dynamo.

Ace Burlington wanders by, missing Doc entirely. Doc
doesn't notice Ace either as he exits and heads in the direction
indicated by an arrowed sign that reads *SECRET ROCKET-
PLANE TEST THIS WAY.*

                                        IRIS WIPE TO:

EXT. FACTORY FRONT GATE – DAY
Outside the gate, at a wooden barricade, Nancy argues with
Pop, while Ricky pretends to drive Nancy's car, a late model
Studebaker. He makes "zooming" and "vroom-ing" sounds as
he spins the wheel.

                              NANCY
Look, I have to get to the test field. It's an
emergency.

POP

Nope. I got my orders. Nobody gets in without a special signed pass. You want me to lose my job? I got a widowed mother to support.

GAMS (O.S.)

Excuse me...

Pop and Nancy turn to see Gams Catling pull up to the front gate in a Desoto. Gams is in disguise, wearing a blonde wig, heavy lipstick, glasses and a school matron's starched dress.

GAMS

I'm from Lou Costello High School. Which way is it to the Rocketplane test?

POP

Down the road to that first hangar on your right.

GAMS

Thank you.

Pop works the gate barricade, and Gams drives through.

NANCY

Why did you let her in?

POP

Heck, now... she's a school teacher.

NANCY

Well, I'm a registered nurse.

POP

Well, why didn't you say so?

He lifts the barricade. Nancy runs to her car, pushes Ricky over and slides behind the wheel.

Nancy looks grim as she drives through the gate at high speed.

> NANCY
> Did you see that woman who just drove in?

> RICKY
> Who, the school teacher?

> NANCY
> No real school teacher would wear that shade of lipstick without a dark base!

> RICKY
> Holy cats, you mean–?

> NANCY
> That school teacher is a floozy! A floozy named Gams Catling!

EXT. AERODROME HANGAR – DAY

A large sign on the hangar reads: *SECRET ROCKETPLANE ENGINE TEST HERE TODAY*. Gams' Desoto pulls around to the rear. Nancy parks her car in front of hangar, out of view of the Desoto. She and Ricky tiptoe to the corner of the hangar...

Nancy and Ricky peek around the corner to find themselves facing Longjohn's chest. They look up. He looks down. Behind Longjohn, Shortie climbs from the trunk of the Desoto, handing Gams a machine gun. He has a machine gun of his own. Ricky yelps, tries to run.

Ricky's feet run frantically without touching the ground. CAMERA PANS UP Ricky to show Longjohn holding him by the collar. Nancy gets off a punch that barely fazes the big man. Then he picks her up, kicking and struggling.

Gams walks up, pulling off her glasses.

> GAMS
> Didn't you hear, kid? School's out.

> NANCY
> You'll laugh out of the other side of your uncolor-coordinated mouth when Doc gets here!

> GAMS
> (startled, breathless)
> Doc Dynamo! He's alive?
> (catching herself)
> Well... too bad for him... the big good-looking lug. And for you.

EXT. AERODROME ROADWAY – DAY
Keppler and Palmer argue as they approach the Rocket-plane hangar.

> PALMER
> I still say you're the traitor! You're a German, aren't you?

> KEPPLER
> Sviss! I keep telling you–I'm Sviss!

> PALMER
> Well, I've got my eye on you, Keppler. If it wasn't for the test about to begin, I'd...

As Palmer speaks, he and Keppler walk into the hangar. From inside a moment later, comes the SOUND OF TWO BLOWS, followed by a HEAVY THUD. Beat; then Shortie peeks his head out door, looks around, beckons back into hangar. Longjohn emerges, unconscious Palmer slung over his shoulder, and carries him around to rear of hangar, as Shortie goes back inside.

INT. AERODROME HANGAR - DAY
No sign of Keppler. Shortie crosses the hangar to the spot where the crates of dynamite have been piled around the single-engine racer to be used for the test. The Rocketplane engine has replaced the propeller and engine in the plane's nose.

Shortie crouches beside the crates, opens one box to reveal the tightly-packed dynamite inside. He pulls out a coiled length of fuse and plays it out, backing up to the door of the hangar. The fuse is 20 feet long. Shortie stands at the door, holding one end of the fuse... and pats his pockets for a match. Doc Dynamo, whom we see standing in the doorway behind him, hands him a lighter.

                    SHORTIE
          Thanks.

Shortie flicks the lighter, about to light the fuse... and slowly does a take, doesn't want to believe it, turning very, very slowly.

SHORTIE'S POV - DOC'S FIST
is cocked, and slams hard INTO CAMERA.

Shortie goes down, and Doc grins, rubbing his knuckle. Suddenly, there's a THUMP, and Doc falls forward stunned... and there's Ace Burlington behind him, holding his Police Special and looking triumphant.

Another beat, another THUMP, and Ace goes down... and there's Longjohn behind him, holding a crowbar. Longjohn takes a quick glance over his own shoulder, then releases as we...

WIPE TO:

EXT. HANGAR (REAR)
Palmer wakes groggily beside the Desoto, and finds himself facing Gams' beautiful legs. He slowly looks up and up and up... into the muzzle of a machine gun. Gams has him covered.

Stepping INTO VIEW beside her is–The Thunder.

> THUNDER
> I hope you like to travel, Mr. Palmer. You're going to see the world.

> PALMER
> (bangs his fist)
> By Godfrey, I've got it–you're The Thunder!

> THUNDER
> And you're my guest. Icarus Aircraft has served its purpose. I have decided it will be easier to destroy the Rocketplane prototype than to smuggle it out... especially when I can bring its Chief Engineer back to the Third Reich, to build a fleet of Rocketplanes for the Fuhrer.

Laughing, The Thunder turns to go. Gams glances toward him, momentarily taking her eyes off Palmer. Palmer lunges to his feet, makes a grab for The Thunder.

PALMER'S HAND yanks off The Thunder's hood.

Palmer, standing with the hood in his hand, astounded by what he sees. The Thunder is OUT OF FRAME.

88

PALMER

You? You're The Thunder? You? But you... you're...
you're... you...

A GUN FIRING once... twice... three times. Four times. Five
times. Six times. Seven times. A dozen times in quick succession.

Palmer looks down at his shirt front in surprise. No visible
sign of a wound. He clutches himself, and slides dead to the
ground, still holding The Thunder's hood.

PALMER
(voice fading as he falls)
... you're... you're... you...

THUNDER'S HOOD
as The Thunder's right hand picks it up, the smoking gun in
his left.

INT. AERODROME HANGAR
Doc wakes groggily to find himself bound hand and foot, his
hands tied in front of him. Beside him, Ace is similarly bound,
unconscious and snoring. Shortie is lighting the fire with
Doc's lighter. Longjohn is busy stacking crates marked *DY-
NAMITE*.

DOC'S BELT
Doc's bound hands pry open the D-shaped belt buckle, press a
stud on the inside–and a pair of scissors extend from within
the belt, cutting the ropes around Doc's wrists with a snip.

Shortie and Longjohn react, sensing someone looking down
on them. They turn to see Doc poised on the wing of the
Rocketplane. He launches himself into the air, somersaulting–
and they jump aside.

He lands between them, as Longjohn swings a crowbar. Doc ducks under the crowbar, which hits Shortie. The fight begins in earnest. Ace snores on as the fuse burns slowly from the door toward the dynamite crates.

EXT. HANGAR (REAR)
Gams checking Palmer's pulse. She looks up at The Thunder, who's adjusting the hood over his head.

>   GAMS
>   He's dead. I thought you wanted to take him back to
>   the Fuhrer?

>   THUNDER
>   A change of plans. No one must ever know the true
>   identity of–The Thunder.

Suddenly, they hear a CRASH ON SOUND from within the hangar.

>   GAMS
>   Something's wrong...

>   THUNDER
>   Take care of it. I'll meet you at our secret hideout.

He runs off, and Gams takes off toward the hangar.

INT. AERODROME HANGAR
Shortie grabs up a smaller crate marked *DYNAMITE*, lifts it overhead to hurl at Doc–then realizes what he's doing and blanches. He sets the crate down like a basket of eggs, starts to tiptoe away.

In a tangle with Longjohn, Doc manages to grab Shortie's foot, and heaves–sends Shortie sliding face-first across the floor, paralleling the burning fuse. Ace snores.

90

Doc and Longjohn struggle, Longjohn trying to choke Doc. Doc breaks his grip and, using a complicated and improbable judo throw, heaves Longjohn overhead. Longjohn crashes into the wing of the plane, head going right through the flimsy balsa wood wing.

Doc turns to find Shortie... and instead, comes face to face with Gams Catling. She has him covered with her machine gun. Doc hesitates–and Longjohn hits Doc over the head with a propeller blade.

Gams takes a last look at stunned Doc, lying by the burning fuse, as she and her mob run out. Ace snores.

> GAMS
> He's so good-looking... but so dumb.

EXT. AERODROME HANGAR - THE DUMPSTER
BANGING and MUFFLED CRIES come from inside the dumpster as Lanton hurries up. In background, Gams' car tears away in a cloud of smoke. Lanton opens the dumpster.

Chislewit and Hooper run up, from opposite directions.

> CHISLEWIT
> Mr. Lanton! Where are Palmer and Keppler? This
> test should have begun ten minutes ago! These delays
> are costing us money!

Chislewit gapes as Nancy climbs from the dumpster, covered with garbage, newspapers, trash.

> NANCY
> Hurry... The Thunder's going to blow up the Rocket-
> plane engine...
> (beat)
> Where's Ricky?

HANGAR FRONT ENTRANCE
Doc staggers from the open door, hand to head, as Nancy and
the others run up. He supports Ace with one hand.

> NANCY
> Doc... the Rocketplane engine... you've got to save
> it...

> DOC
> I really have to get a thicker helmet...

> LANTON
> The Rocketplane, man! The Rocketplane!

> NANCY
> Doc, it's going to explode!

> RICKY (O.S.)
> Don't worry, Doc!

Ricky's VOICE comes from inside the hangar. All turn, gaping.

INT. ROCKETPLANE HANGAR - THEIR POV
Ricky inside the hangar, running toward the burning fuse, only
a foot from the crates of dynamite.

> RICKY
> I'll get it!

He stamps on the fuse–and burns his foot. The fuse burns on
as Ricky hops back, clutching his foot, howling: "Owwwww!"
Hopping about on one foot, Ricky gets his other leg caught
between two crates. Tries to pull it free–can't. He turns toward
the watchers outside–shrugs.

EXT. ROCKETPLANE HANGAR

DOC
Someday I'm going to kill that kid.

He runs into the hangar.

LANTON
Save the engine!

NANCY
No–save Ricky!

INT. ROCKETPLANE HANGAR
Ricky's trying unsuccessfully to pull his foot free, but can't.

NARRATOR
Only you can decide! Should Doc save the
Rocketplane engine, last best hope of democracy–

SUPERED LEGEND ON SCREEN: *SAVE THE ROCKET-
PLANE ENGINE?*

NARRATOR (cont'd)
–Or should he risk all to rescue little Ricky one
more time?

SUPERED LEGEND ON SCREEN: *OR–SAVE RICKY
AGAIN?*

NARRATOR (cont'd)
To learn which choice you make–

EXT. NEW JERSEY AERODROME - LONG SHOT
as the Rocketplane hangar EXPLODES TREMENDOUSLY,
wood and steel flying through the air in graceful slow motion.

93

                    NARRATOR
              (as SOUND OF EXPLOSION
                  recedes slightly)
–don't miss the fourth exciting chapter of–"Doc Dynamo!"

SUPERED TITLE: *"Don't miss CHAPTER FOUR: HUMAN
TARGET!"*

                              FADE OUT.

FADE IN:

TITLE CARD: *"DOC DYNAMO–America's Ace Spy-Swatter."* Minimal credits, TRIUMPHAL MUSIC, followed by (on a DOWN NOTE):

TITLE CARD: *"CHAPTER FOUR: HUMAN TARGET!"*

WIPE TO:

(NOTE: *CHAPTER OPENS WITH A REPRISE OF THE MOVIETOWN NEWSREEL, AND EDITED FOOTAGE FROM THE PREVIOUS CHAPTER'S CLIFFHANGER, END-ING WITH...*)

EXT. HANGAR
Doc suddenly brightens, as if a lightbulb had just gone on over his head. He runs OUT OF FRAME–

CHOICE #1: SAVE THE ENGINE

INT. HANGAR
Doc runs in, and toward Ricky. Ricky smiles; Doc's come to rescue him! But to the boy's amazement, Doc runs right past him.

Doc reaches the plane. Frantically, he pushes a locking bolt– and a huge clamp that holds the engine in place falls away.

Doc scrambles up into the fuselage, looks into cockpit area.

INT. COCKPIT - CLOSE
Zillions of dials, clocks, gauges, etc. DOC'S HAND REACHES INTO FRAME–and flicks one teensy-tiny switch in the middle.

INT. HANGAR
The engine ROARS TO LIFE.

The fuse is burning nearer to the dynamite.

Doc scrambles out of cockpit. Teeth gritted, he looks at the prototype–and the burning fuse.

He pulls at Ricky's leg–can't get it free. He looks down.

DOC'S POV - RICKY'S FOOT
clearly seen to be turned at an angle that *keeps* it caught.

> DOC
> (slowly, patiently)
> Ricky... son... turn your foot halfway around.

Ricky, puzzled, looks down...

DOC'S & RICKY'S POV - RICKY'S FOOT
turns 90 degrees... no longer caught by the crates.

> RICKY
> Wow! You're the greatest, Doc!

CHOICE #2: SAVE RICKY!

INT. HANGAR
Doc runs in, and toward Ricky. Ricky smiles; Doc's come to rescue him!

Doc, teeth gritted, looks at the prototype–and the burning fuse.

He pulls at Ricky's leg–can't get it free. He looks down.

DOC'S POV - RICKY'S FOOT
clearly seen to be turned at an angle that *keeps* it caught.

                    DOC
              (slowly, patiently)
        Ricky... son... turn your foot halfway around.

Ricky, puzzled, looks down...

DOC'S & RICKY'S POV - RICKY'S FOOT
turns 90 degrees... no longer caught by the crates.

                    RICKY
        Wow! You're the greatest, Doc!

Doc reaches the plane. Frantically he pushes a locking bolt–
and a huge clamp that holds the engine in place falls away.

Doc scrambles up into the fuselage, looks into cockpit area.

INT. COCKPIT - CLOSE
Zillions of dials, clocks, gauges, etc. DOC'S HAND
REACHES INTO FRAME–and flicks one teensy-tiny switch
in the middle.

INT. HANGAR
The engine ROARS TO LIFE.

(*FOOTAGE FROM CHOICES #1 & #2 COMBINE HERE.*)

The fuse is only an inch away now from the dynamite crate.

Doc climbs onto the prototype, to straddle the now-throbbing,
nigh-deafening engine between his legs, as Ricky watches
open-mouthed. Doc reaches out his hand toward Ricky, shouts
over the ROAR.

                    DOC
        Come on, Ricky! This thing's our ticket out of here!

Doc pulls him up behind him on top of the ROARING EN-
GINE

INT. HANGAR
The Rocketplane Engine suddenly ZOOMS away from rest of
plane, with Doc and Ricky on it.

EXT. HANGAR
The Rocketplane Engine carries Doc and Ricky out of the
hangar, ten feet off the ground. Doc grim; Ricky waving his
arms wildly about.

                        RICKY
        Wa-hooo!

Nancy, Ace, Lanton, Chislewit and Hooper look up in aston-
ishment, from left to right, reacting as the shadow of the engine falls over them–

EXT. AERODROME FIELD
The engine imbeds itself with a SPLOP! in the soft earth of a
low hillock, just beyond a higher one. Doc and Ricky thrown
off, and roll over and over, finally coming to a stop. They
scramble to their feet, as Nancy, Ace, Lanton, Chislewit and
Hooper run up.

INT. HANGAR
The fuse finally reaches the dynamite crate–a second's
SPUTTERING–

EXT. HANGAR
EXPLODES with a thunderous ROAR, wood and steel flying
through the air in graceful slow motion.

EXT. HILLOCK
Doc raises his head from behind hillock. So do the others, one
by one.

RICKY

Wow! What a blow-up!

DOC

That's not a very respectful attitude to have toward
other people's private property, young man.

Ricky hangs his head sheepishly for a moment. But as soon as
Doc looks back toward the explosion, he stares wide-eyed
again, a wide smile on his face. The others follow around the
hillock, cautiously. Ace rubs his head, suspiciously.

ACE

Maybe I was wrong about you, Doc.
        (with emphasis)
Maybe.

DOC

Mr. Lanton, this gives me an idea. Only we know that
the Rocketplane engine survived that explosion. If
The Thunder tries to steal it again, that'll prove for
certain that one of you four Board members is a traitor—

LANTON

—because only we know the Rocketplane still exists!
        (looks around)
Wait a minute! Four? Say, where are Keppler—and
Palmer? They were supposed to be here, too!

CHISLEWIT

That proves that one of them is The Thunder!

Keppler limps around the corner, holding his head and moan-
ing.

LANTON

Grab him!

Doc and Nancy grab Keppler.

KEPPLER

Vot der devil are you doing?

RICKY

Capturing The Thunder, that's what!

He kicks Keppler in shin; the scientist yowls, staggers.

KEPPLER

Vot are you talking about? Der Tunder's men bopped
me on der cranium. Look!

He points to bump on head.

HOOPER

That bump looks pretty genuine, Mr. Lanton.

LANTON

Shut up, Hooper. If I need a male secretary's
opinion, I'll ask for it.
(looks at it)
It does look pretty real, though, doesn't it?
(spins around)
Then where's Palmer? The Thunder must be–my own
Chief Engineer!

Ace stands gesturing by a corner of another building.

ACE

Uh–Mr. Lanton, sir... if you could step over here a
moment...

Lanton leads the way, grumbling; Doc and others follow, no longer holding Keppler. Ace points around the corner.

THEIR POV - PALMER
lying dead. Still clutching himself, no sign of a wound.

Nancy pushes her way forward. She crouches beside the body, as Doc holds Ricky back so he can't rush forward for a better look.

                    NANCY
          Stand back. I'm a registered nurse!
                    (a beat)
          He's been shot.
                    (feels pulse)
          I'd say he's been dead about half an hour.
                    (looks at wrist)
          And his watch is slow.

                    ACE
          Well... I guess that lets him off the hook as a suspect.

                    DOC
          Then that must mean it's one of you three men.

                    HOOPER
                    (scribbling in notebook)
          "... one of you three men..."

Doc looks intently at Lanton, Keppler and Chislewit. Each of them looks guilty, guilty, guilty.

                                        WIPE TO:

EXT. WATERFRONT AREA - NIGHT - (STOCK) (1940)

EXT. THUNDER'S SHACK - NIGHT
Sitting at the very end of a wharf is The Thunder's shack. A shadowy figure makes his way down the wharf, stepping on an unseen cat's tail. The cat leaps away with a HOWL.

> THUNDER
> (entering shack)
> Verdammte pussycat.

INT. THE THUNDER'S SECRET LAB – NIGHT
Light comes on. The Thunder activates Tele-Visor; Hitler appears.

> THUNDER
> (sieg-heiling)
> Heil Hitler! Mein Fuhrer, I have good news and–

He's about to say "bad."

> HITLER
> You better not have any bad news this time.

> THUNDER
> –and better news. The good news is that the Rocket-plane engine is still in American hands.

> HITLER
> That is the good news?

> THUNDER
> And the better news is that Doc Dynamo has sworn to capture and unmask me at all costs!

> HITLER
> That is the better news?

THUNDER

Of course, Mein Fuhrer. Now, it will be simplicity itself to lure the famous Doc Dynamo into a trap and
destroy him–and then the Rocketplane engine prototype will be ours for the taking!

HITLER
(long beat; thinks about it)
Ja... that sounds reasonable. Good work, Thunder.
Heil Hitler!

The Thunder salutes and CLICKS OFF Tele-Visor hurriedly,
turns TOWARD CAMERA and turns his salute into a brow-
wiping.

THUNDER

Whew!

WIPE TO:

INT. DR. FRED'S INNER OFFICE – DAY
Dr. Fred and Nancy pour over charts as Ace suddenly bursts
in, a pair of handcuffs swinging from his left coat pocket. Dr.
Fred and Nancy react in surprise.

NANCY
Why, Inspector Burlington–
(before he can correct her)
–Ace–what are you doing here?

ACE
Don't be coy with me, Nurse Wallace. I've come
about Doc Dynamo. Where is he?

He looks around office, under tables, etc.

NANCY

I told you before, I don't know anything about him.

ACE
(his face close to hers)

You don't, huh? So how come you seem to show up
wherever he shows up–he's always saving the lives
of you and that bratty brother of yours–his special
car's been seen coming out of the garage of
this very building–
(as she starts to speak; he turns on
Dr. Fred)
–and he's exactly the same height, weight and skin
tone as Dr. Fred Franklin!

DR. FRED

Y-you think I'm Doc Dynamo?

ACE

I'm not sure–but they're on my back at city hall for
me to crack this Thunder case wide open, or I'll be
pounding a beat in the Bronx. With my head.
(strides to door)
From now on, Dr. Fred, I'm keeping my eye on you.
Where you go–Ace Burlington goes!

He stomps out.

NANCY

Sounds like trouble.

DR. FRED

We'll blow up that bridge when we come to it. Right
now, Nurse Wallace, I want to show you something
important.

He strides into his inner sanctum. Nancy doesn't follow, not being particularly impressed by Dr. Fred. After a beat, the deeper, more masculine voice of Doc Dynamo calls from the sanctum.

                    DOC (O.S.)
          Nurse Wallace–if you don't mind?

                    NANCY
               (her eyes glazed)
          Doc Dynamo?

In a daze, she rushes into the sanctum.

INT. DOC'S INNER SANCTUM – DAY
Inside, Nancy comes face to face with Dr. Fred. She looks crestfallen that he's not in his Doc Dynamo uniform.

                    NANCY
          You tricked me! You're still Dr. Fred!

                    DOC
               (pointedly)
          Forgive me, Nurse Wallace, but I needed your atten-
          tion.

Dr. Fred opens the doors of the cabinet containing his Tele-Visor, and activates the machine as Nancy looks on.

Wavy line patterns crisscross the screen, followed by a HIGH HUMMING... which cuts off abruptly as the screen clears. Nancy gasps in surprise.

                    NANCY
          Dr. Fred... isn't that–?

ANGLE - DR. FRED & TELE-VISOR

On the Tele-Visor: A German U-boat cruising out to sea.

> DOC
> A German U-Boat, cruising three miles off shore, in
> international waters.
>> (beat)
> I'm betting The Thunder and his mob plan to steal
> the Rocketplane and ship it to Germany aboard that
> submarine.

> NANCY
> Shouldn't we alert the Coast Guard?

> DR. FRED
> No time. I've told Dr. Keppler to move the Rocket-
> plane to a new, safe, secret location in the
> Poconos–

> NANCY
> Dr. Keppler! Suppose he's The Thunder? He is Ger-
> man, after all!

> DR. FRED
>> (smiling)
> Swiss, Nancy. Swiss.
>> (serious)
> Now, if I'm going to throw Inspector Burlington off
> the scent, we have to act fast. It's a good thing your
> kid brother isn't around to make things worse–

They turn from the Tele-Visor to see Ricky standing half a
foot behind them, grinning and eager.

> RICKY
>> (staring at Tele-Visor)
> Wow! That's a heckuva home movie outfit you got,
> Dr. Fred!

Dr. Fred and Nurse Nancy exchange long-suffering looks.

                              WIPE TO:

EXT. EMPIRE STATE BUILDING - DAY
Ace leans against his police car, handcuffs sticking prominently out of his coat pocket. Looks up from a *Black Mask
Detective* pulp as Dr. Fred and Ricky emerge through the front
door. Each has a fishing pole. Ricky sticks close by Dr. Fred,
much to latter's annoyance.

                         DR. FRED
             Good evening, Commissioner.

                          RICKY
             Dr. Fred's taking me fishing!

He waves his pole.

                           ACE
                      (suspiciously)
             Oh yeah? Then I hope you've got a third pole up your
             sleeve, Dr. Fred, alias Doc Dynamo—'cause I'm
             sticking to you like glue.

Suddenly, with a LOUD ROAR ON SOUND, White Lightning zooms by, with what seems to be Doc Dynamo behind
the wheel. Ace whirls, amazed.

                          RICKY
                  (much mugging and winking)
             Hiya, Doc! Hiya!
                      RICKY (cont'd)
                        (to Ace)
             Doc Dynamo's a personal friend of mine,
             Inspector Ace!

                    ACE
              (double-takes; to Dr. Fred)
        I must've been out of my mind, thinking you were
        him.
              (hops into his car)
        Doc Dynamo, here I come!

POLICE CAR PEELS OUT, Dr. Fred and Ricky looking after.

                  DR. FRED
        Well, Ricky, that was a fine joke you helped me pull,
        and I'm sure that if Doc Dynamo were here, he'd ap-
        preciate it as much as I do. But I've got to be going
        now, so I guess this is where you and I part company.

Ricky just grins–lifts one hand to show that he and Dr. Fred
are handcuffed together with Ace's own cuffs... Ricky's left to
Dr. Fred's right.

                    RICKY
        Where you go, I go. Some fun, huh, Dr. Fred?

EXT. NEW YORK STREET - DAY
White Lightning CAREENS around a corner, speeds into the
night...

INT. WHITE LIGHTNING - DAY
Behind the wheel: Nurse Nancy, wearing the flight outfit,
helmet and goggles of Doc Dynamo. They don't fit very well,
and the helmet is loose enough that she has to keep pushing
the goggles out of her eyes. She looks into the rear view mirror...

HER POV - REAR VIEW MIRROR
Ace's police car, SIREN WAILING, just a couple of car
lengths behind her.

EXT. COUNTRY ROAD - DAY
White Lightning zooms by, followed by Ace's car, SIREN ON
SOUND.

ZIP WIPE TO:

EXT. ICARUS AIRCRAFT COMPANY - DAY
BINOCULAR VIEW of the factory grounds (from Chapter
One), where Dr. Keppler can be seen supervising the loading
of the Rocketplane into the rear of a covered truck by two
husky factory workers.

> GAMS (O.S.)
> Looks like you had it figured three ways from Sun-
> day, Thunder...

EXT. HILLSIDE (OUTSIDE FACTORY) - DAY
Gams and the Thunder crouch on a hillside overlooking the
Icarus factory; Gams peers through a pair of binoculars at the
factory below. The Thunderwagon is parked prominently in
the background.

> GAMS
> They're moving the Rocketplane engine, just like you
> said. Shortie and Longjohn are already in position, so
> this'll be a piece of cake.
> (a long beat)
> Promise me one thing, will you? If Doc Dynamo gets
> in our way... don't hurt him.

> THUNDER
> You surprise me, Gams.

> GAMS
> I know what you're going to say. A girl like me... a
> guy like him. I know it's hopeless. I know I don't

GAMS (cont'd)
stand a chance. But I love the guy, you hear? Sure, as
far as he knows, I'm just a no-good two-bit floozy.
Next to him, I'm nothing... a nobody... a piece of dirt
under his boot... A tart, a bimbo, a cheap twist.
(mad as hell)
Say, who the hell does he think he is, anyway?
(grabs her gun)
That stuck-up son of a bitch, I'll kill him!

The Thunder looks heavenward as we:

WIPE TO:

EXT. DESERTED HILL ROAD – DAY
A sign by the side of the road reads: *TUNNEL AHEAD*. Hast-
ily painted, paint running slightly. Sign is caught briefly in a
flare of headlights as Keppler's TRUCK RUMBLES PAST.

INT. KEPPLER'S TRUCK CAB - DAY
Keppler and two brawny factory workers sit crowded in the
cab.

INT. TRUCK REAR COMPARTMENT - DAY
The Rocketplane engine sways in its restraining harness.

EXT. DESERTED HILL ROAD
The truck heads toward a sheer cliff wall ahead, broken by a
black tunnel entrance that seems strangely one-dimensional in
headlight beams.

ROADSIDE DITCH
Shortie and Longjohn crouch in a ditch as the TRUCK
ROARS BY. Shortie smothers a snicker. Beside them in the
ditch is a large can of black paint and several wet paint
brushes. A moment after the truck goes by, A LOUD

110

SCREECHING AND CRASHING ON SOUND shatters the night. Shortie and Longjohn clamber from the ditch.

Shortie runs up to Keppler's truck, which has crashed head-first into the sheer face of the cliff: the "tunnel" was only painted on. The front end of the truck is squeezed up like an accordion, the truck cab is completely flattened. Keppler's arm sticks from the tangled wreckage. Shortie checks his pulse, and makes a cutting motion across his throat: Dr. Keppler's dead.

A SECOND TRUCK backs INTO FRAME, driven by Longjohn. He and Shortie proceed to transfer the Rocketplane engine from the wrecked truck to the new truck.

                                                    WIPE TO:

EXT. COUNTRY ROAD INTERSECTION - DAY
A lonely intersection with a three-way switch-light. The White Lightning ROARS to a stop before a red light. Ace pulls up on White Lightning's right.

Ace glances over at "Doc"–and does a double-take.

ACE'S POV - "Doc" waves at him prettily, blows him a kiss.

Ace sputters with surprise.

Nancy/"Doc" grins... and suddenly her grin fades as she sees:

NANCY'S POV - THE INTERSECTION
Longjohn and Shortie drive through the intersection at high speed. As their truck passes by, the Rocketplane engine can be glimpsed in the open end of the truck, half-covered by a tarp.

Nancy does a take, instantly floors gas pedal, spinning the wheel.

White Lightning zooms after the receding truck, spitting up a cloud of dust that completely covers the Inspector's car.

Ace, coughing and choking in the thick dust cloud, is totally blind. He floors the gas pedal, car zooming OUT OF FRAME. Half a second later, we hear a TREMENDOUS CRASHING O.S.

Ace's car stands on its nose, wheels spinning, having crashed head-first into the traffic light.

EXT. COUNTRY ROAD – DAY
The truck sweeps by, followed by White Lightning.

INT. TRUCK CAB – DAY
Shortie and Longjohn see White Lightning's headlights in their rearview mirror, and wink at each other broadly. Shortie speaks into a large broadcast-style microphone.

                    SHORTIE
        Break out the welcome wagon, boss. Just like you
        figured... Doc Dynamo's on our tail!

                    WIPE TO:

EXT. WATERFRONT – DAY
Handcuffed together, Dr. Fred and Ricky walk down a foggy waterfront street past saloons with swinging signs above their doors that read: *THE DIRTY DOG, THE DIRTY RAT, THE DIRTY DUCK*.

                  DR. FRED
       This is a dirty neighborhood, Ricky.

RICKY

You think we'll find The Thunder's hideout down
here, Dr. Fred?

DR. FRED

It stands to reason. The Thunder has a submarine
waiting off shore to pick up the Rocketplane engine
prototype. He's got to have a hideout somewhere on
the waterfront. We just have to find it.

WIPE TO:

EXT. ACME WAREHOUSE – DAY

White Lightning rolls up slowly, headlights spearing the darkness. The truck she's been following is parked under a sign
reading "*ACME MEAT STORAGE.*"

Nancy parks and climbs out. She checks the rear of the truck,
sees the Rocketplane engine sitting inside, shakes her head,
puzzled. Cautiously, she approaches the warehouse door...

INT. WAREHOUSE – DAY

The Thunder crouches with Gams, Shortie, Longjohn behind a
bunch of crates. Shortie brandishes a sub-machine gun.

SHORTIE

So as soon as Doc Dynamo pokes his head in, we
blast 'im, right, boss?

THUNDER

(slaps him)
No, you fool. That would be too easy–too crude a
way to destroy the great Doc Dynamo. I have a better
plan.

SHORTIE

Yeah? What is it?

113

                    THUNDER
          Step out there and see.

He gestures to the corridor between themselves and the door.

                    SHORTIE
          Who, me?

                    THUNDER
          What's wrong, Shortie? Don't you trust me?

Shortie's glance tells us he sure as hell doesn't. But he can't
refuse. Even Longjohn is gesturing him to do it. Timidly,
Shortie rises and walks out to the middle of a long, narrow
corridor formed by crates piled nearly to the ceiling. Slabs of
meat dangle from meat-hooks on an overhead rack down the
center of the corridor. The warehouse entrance is at one end of
the corridor.

The Thunder pulls a lever in the floor, as Gams reacts.

INT. WAREHOUSE - SHORTIE'S FEET
Suddenly, at Shortie's feet, a hidden trapdoor drops open–and
some yards below, churning dark waters can be seen. Shortie
teeters a moment on the edge, recovers his balance.

                    SHORTIE
          Whoa.

SHORTIE'S POV - THE WATERS BELOW

A shark's fin knifes through the water, accompanied by
"Jaws"-like THEME MUSIC.

                    SHORTIE
          I think there's some kind'a fish down there.

                         THUNDER
     Very astute.

Thunder works the lever, to a halfway point.

The trapdoor swings shut, forming an almost seamless seal.

                         THUNDER
                       (chortling)
     That trapdoor is set to open at the slightest pressure.
     One step will plunge Doc Dynamo through to a wa-
     tery grave.

Laughing, The Thunder moves off with Shortie and Longjohn... as Gams lingers behind, looking at the trapdoor with
concern...

EXT. WAREHOUSE
Nancy/"Doc" cautiously edges her way to the open doorway.
Looks in.

NANCY'S POV - THE WAREHOUSE seems deserted, all
the way down that long, lonely single aisle.

Nancy goes inside.

INT. WAREHOUSE
Nancy starts warily down the corridor of crates. BOARDS
CREAK under her feet. She ducks around swinging meat-
slabs, peering cautiously from side to side as she proceeds
down the corridor. She pays more attention to the meat-slabs
before and above her than to where she's stepping.

NANCY'S FEET
She stops just an inch away from the closed trapdoor.

Nancy starts forward again—

NANCY'S FEET
—about to step onto the waiting trap.

> GAMS (O.S.)
> Doc, look out!

Nancy whirls, as Gams Catling steps INTO VIEW, behind her. Gams' look of concern changes to a hostile sneer.

> GAMS
> You're not Dynamo...

A silver-plated .45 appears in her hand. Nancy tries to brazen it out with a deep voice.

> NANCY
> How can you tell?

Gams steps forward for a closer look in the darkness.

> GAMS
> Sister—if you're Doc Dynamo, I'm Bugs Bunny.
> (grins)
> What's up, Doc?

> NANCY
> Not much—except you've got a run in your stocking.

> GAMS
> Where?

In spite of herself, Gams looks down and Nancy jumps at her, swinging a terrific uppercut. Gams staggers backward, her gun falling behind a crate. Nancy follows with a roundhouse left.

Gams gets her wind and slams a powerful right into Nancy's stomach.

EXT. WAREHOUSE
Thunder, Shortie and Longjohn have reached their truck.

> SHORTIE
> Wait a sec... where's Gams?

From within the warehouse, O.S. CRASH, sounds of FIGHT-ING.

> THUNDER
> Forget her. We have the Rocketplane to think about.

Leaping into the truck, they back it up to smash the rear of White Lightning, and then drive off, laughing maniacally.

INT. WAREHOUSE CORRIDOR
Nancy and Gams trade punches toe-to-toe like boxers. There's absolutely nothing "feminine" about the way they fight. Gams plows into Nancy with a five-blow combination, gasping between swings.

> GAMS
> Doc... must think... you're something special! Let's see... what he thinks of you... after this!

Gams gets Nancy with a powerful hook, and Nancy stumbles backward–

NANCY'S FOOT
touches the trapdoor, which springs open. SPLISHING AND SPLASHING O.S. from below.

WATERS BELOW
The shark's fin again–appropriate SINISTER MUSIC.

Nancy dodges an attempted knockout punch, comes back at Gams with two left jabs, a right to the body, a left.

> NANCY
> You... cheap... hussy! No matter what happens... to me... Doc would never look twice... at you!

> GAMS
> Oh yeah?

Body blow.

> NANCY
> Yeah!

> GAMS
> We'll just see about that!

Gams' uppercut sends Nancy reeling–

OPEN TRAPDOOR
Nancy's feet tottering on the edge

WATERS BELOW
STOCK FOOTAGE of a huge, vicious OCTOPUS beneath the water, with appropriate SINISTER MUSIC.

Nancy loses her balance, grabs for Gams–and they both fall across the open trapdoor.

WATERS BELOW
STOCK FOOTAGE of ALLIGATORS, churning in the water, their jaws gaping skyward. Appropriate menacing MUSIC.

Nancy and Gams hang from the trapdoor, side by side, over the churning water. Gams' grip is slipping. Nancy can barely hold on.

> GAMS

> Help me...

> NANCY
> (grip slipping)
> Are you crazy?

> GAMS
> Be a sport. What would Doc do?

Nancy is struck by this thought: What would Doc do?

> NARRATOR (O.S.)
> Should Nurse Nancy Wallace risk her own life to save Gams Catling? The choice is yours...
> (beat)
> Should she save herself–

SUPERED LEGEND ON SCREEN: "*SAVE YOURSELF...*"

Gams bats her eyes, trying hard to look deserving as her grip slips...

> NARRATOR (cont'd)
> –or should she save Gams Catling?

SUPERED LEGEND ON SCREEN: "*...OR SAVE GAMS CATLING?*"

ANGLE - WATERS BELOW
A terrific SPLASH as some large object lands in the water.

ANGLE - BELOW WATERS

STOCK FOOTAGE of a school of fearsome PIRANHAS, swarming all over an unseen object. Appropriate SINISTER MUSIC.

> NARRATOR (cont'd)
> (portentous)
> To learn what choice you make, tune in next week at this time for the last and final episode in the adventures of–"*Doc Dynamo!*"

SUPERED TITLE CARD: *"DON'T MISS CHAPTER FIVE - VICTORY?"*

FADE OUT.

FADE IN:

TITLE CARD: *"DOC DYNAMO–America's Ace Spy-Swatter."* Minimal credits, triumphal MUSIC, followed by (on a down note):

TITLE CARD: *"CHAPTER FIVE: VICTORY?"*

WIPE TO:

(NOTE: *CHAPTER OPENS WITH A REPRISE OF THE MOVIETOWN NEWSREEL, AND EDITED FOOTAGE FROM THE PREVIOUS CHAPTER'S CLIFFHANGER, END-ING WITH...*)

INT. WAREHOUSE CORRIDOR
Nancy and Gams hang from the trapdoor, side by side, over the churning water. Gams' grip is slipping. Nancy can barely hold on. Gams bats her eyes, trying hard to look deserving as her grip slips.

WATERS BELOW
STOCK FOOTAGE of ALLIGATORS, churning in the water, their jaws gaping skyward. Appropriate menacing MUSIC.

CHOICE #1: SAVE HERSELF

Nancy, straining, makes a terrific effort–and comes somersaulting up out of the open trapdoor, spinning in mid-air to land on her feet.

Nancy looks down at the doom that nearly befell her.

Gams gives a scream as her grip fails, and she drops.

Her wrist is caught by Nancy's hand.

CHOICE #2: SAVE GAMS CATLING

Nancy, straining, makes a terrific effort—

—Gams gives a scream as her grip fails, and she drops.

Her wrist is caught by Nancy's hand.

Nancy is holding Gams with one hand and the edge of the trapdoor with the other, starts to pull herself up. Heroically, she pulls herself out of the trapdoor—with one hand!

(*FOOTAGE FROM CHOICES #1 & #2 COMBINE HERE.*)

Gams, pulling on Nancy's hand, is drawn up out of the open trapdoor, breathless on the floor. Her fallen gun lies inches from her hand.

> GAMS
> T-Thanks... you saved my life...
> (grabs the gun)
> ... sucker!

Gams aims at Nancy—who dives behind a slab of meat hanging from a hook, as the GUN ROARS, firing again and again and again.

Nancy, holding the meat slab as a shield, gets close to Gams, who continues to FIRE vainly. Again and again and again. Nancy slams the meat slab into Gams. Gams goes down, unconscious. Nancy tosses the slab aside—into the trapdoor.

WATERS BELOW
A terrific SPLASH as some large object lands in the water. STOCK FOOTAGE of a school of fearsome PIRANHAS, swarming all over an unseen object. Appropriate sinister MU-SIC.

NANCY
(catching her breath)
I don't care if I do love him. I've gotta ask for a raise.

WIPE TO:

EXT. WATERFRONT – DAY
Still handcuffed together, Dr. Fred and Ricky walk through the fog past old warehouses on dock. Suddenly, we hear a continuous BEEP-BEEP-BEEPING from inside Dr. Fred's medical bag... continues ON SOUND through following dialogue.

RICKY
Whazzat noise, Dr. Fred?

DR. FRED
(solemnly)
Ricky... son... because you handcuffed us together like this, you've left me no choice. There's something I must reveal to you that will surprise you–startle you–something you would never have imagined in your wildest dreams. Brace yourself, lad.

Dr. Fred looks around to be sure they're alone. Then he sets the bag down, takes out a portable Tele-Visor ... turns off the BEEPer.

DR. FRED (cont'd)
Dr. Fred Franklin, eminent pediatrician, is, in reality... Doc Dynamo.

RICKY
(feigning shock badly)
No. Really?
(rolls his eyes)

123

Dr. Fred works a few dials on the Tele-Visor and Nancy's image appears. She's back in his secret room, dressed in her nurse's uniform.

                    RICKY
               (yelling, waving)
          Hi, Sis! Can ya hear me, Sis? Hey, guess what! Dr.
          Fred finally spilled the beans about his bein' Doc
          Dynamo!

SPLIT SCREEN - NANCY AND DR. FRED

                    NANCY
          Doc—you told Ricky?

                    DR. FRED
               (chuckles)
          Don't worry, Nurse Wallace. The boy has a strong,
          healthy heart. The shock shouldn't do any permanent
          damage to his cardiovascular system.

                    NANCY
          I guess not. Well, anyway—a couple of things have
          happened around here, too. The Thunder's recaptured
          the RocketPlane engine prototype—

                    RICKY
          What? Again?

                    NANCY (cont'd)
          —and, uh, oh yes, Dr. Keppler's dead.

                    DR. FRED
          But that means—Keppler couldn't have been
          The Thunder.

NANCY

Probably not.
    (grins, gestures over her shoulder)
But maybe our luck is changing. I caught a prisoner.

Behind her, Gams Catling is roped, gagged and blind-folded.

DR. FRED
    (thinking fast)
Good work, Nancy. Darn good work. Get over to the
Icarus Aircraft office, and take your prisoner with
you. I'll meet you there.

NANCY

As Dr. Fred?

DR. FRED

No, Nancy. Dr. Fred's work is done. This is a job
for–
    (deeper voice)
–Doc Dynamo.

NANCY
    (sighs)
I just love it when you do that.
    (recovers)
Nurse Nancy Wallace, over and out.

As the Tele-Visor goes blank, Dr. Fred starts rummaging
around in his medical bag. He brings forth an extra Doc Dynamo outfit, complete with goggles. It's all wadded up, wrin-
kled.

RICKY
Wow! Your Doc Dynamo outfit!

DR. FRED
(looks at cuffs on him and Ricky)
A spare, actually. It'll be tricky, but I think we can manage this. Are you game, son?

RICKY

You bet!

Dr. Fred starts trying to climb into his Doc Dynamo outfit.

WIPE TO:

EXT. ICARUS AIRCRAFT BUILDING - DAY

INT. ICARUS AIRCRAFT BOARDROOM - CLOSE ON LANTON

LANTON
(grim)
Gentlemen... we've got to do something.

CAMERA PULLS BACK to reveal only Lanton and Chislewit around huge conference table. Hooper still taking notes, several feet away. The boardroom window has been replaced.

CHISLEWIT
What do you mean, "Gentlemen"? There's nobody left alive but the two of us.
(Hooper coughs slightly)
And you, too, of course, Hooper.
(to Lanton)
We might as well declare bankruptcy right now, before The Thunder kills us as well.

LANTON
But you forget, Chislewit—one of the two of us is The Thunder.

Their eyes shift nervously from side to side.

Suddenly, the office door opens–and Nurse Nancy walks in, with Gams Catling in tow.

> LANTON (cont'd)
> Nurse Wallace... what's the meaning of this?

A SUDDEN CRASHING from the direction of the window–all react as Doc comes swinging in... and with him, still hand-cuffed to Doc's wrist, is Ricky. They catch their balance awkwardly.

> GAMS
> (breathless)
> Doc Dynamo.

> DOC
> (briskly)
> I'll be happy to explain, Mr. Lanton...

Doc wears his helmet, goggles and uniform–but his Dynamo jacket is hopelessly tangled between him and Ricky.

> DOC (cont'd)
> Nurse Wallace, wait outside... I want to execute Plan Triple B.

> NANCY
> (confused)
> Plan Triple B?

> DOC
> (winks, nods at Gams)
> Right. Plan Triple B.

NANCY
(gets it)
Oh. Plan Triple B. I thought for a second you said
Plan Triple Z. Right, Doc. I'll be outside this door.
Right outside this door. No problem.

She goes out, pushing Gams ahead of her. Doc turns trium-
phantly to Lanton and Chislewit, glass crunching underfoot.

CHISLEWIT
I hope you'll tell us what's going on. These delays
cost money.

As Doc talks, Ricky looks around the room, impressed. He
sees a notepad on the conference table near Hooper, picks it
up idly, looking through it. Frowns, and slips the pad in his
pocket, unnoticed by the others.

DOC
Gentlemen, I believe The Thunder plans to transfer
the Rocketplane to a German U-Boat lurking off
shore... this very night.

LANTON
Good Lord!

CHISLEWIT
Can he be stopped?

DOC
First, we have to locate The Thunder's secret headquarters. That woman out there is the notorious mob
moll known as Gams Catling. She works for The
Thunder.
(others gasp)
If anyone knows the location of his secret headquarters, she does.

> LANTON

Can you make her talk?

> DOC

There's no time. I have another plan.

Ricky, listening with increasing interest, now snaps his fingers.

> RICKY

Plan Triple B! Wow! Sis is gonna let her escape...
and then you'll track her in White Lightning, straight
to The Thunder's secret lab!

> DOC

You know, Ricky... you're quite a bright young lad.

> LANTON

Will it work?

> DOC

What could go wrong?

The door bursts open and Ace Burlington barges in, dragging a kicking, struggling Gams Catling.

> ACE

Hey, Dynamo... Good thing I was on my way up
here. I recognized this pretty little piece of goods and
arrested her.

Nurse Nancy appears in the doorway behind Ace, gives Doc a hopeless shrug. Gams, spotting Doc, stares at him, love-struck.

> DOC

Inspector Burlington, what incredible luck.

                              ACE
Call me Ace.
                    (to Nancy)
I'm gonna run this dame down to the Hall of Justice.
How's about you and me catching a matinee after-
ward?

                            NANCY
Ace... for the last time... get it through that thick
block of cement you call a skull... I'm never going
out with you. Never. Ever. Never.

                              ACE
                    (grins, to Ricky)
Women. They love playin' hard to get.

Nancy stifles a scream of frustration. Ace leaves with Gams in
tow. She can't take her eyes off Doc as the door shuts behind
them.

                            NANCY
Doc, there's still a chance for Plan Triple B.

                              DOC
                    (dejected)
What chance? Triple B requires an escaped prisoner.

                            RICKY
                    (equally dejected)
Yeah. What chance does Gams Catling have to get
free from Inspector Ace?

He and Doc do a slow take... and then rush for the door. The
three of them get wedged before Nancy slips through, then
Doc, then Ricky. Back at the table, Lanton and Chislewit exchange hopeless looks.

                              130

WIPE TO:

EXT. ICARUS AIRCRAFT BUILDING – DAY

Doc, Ricky and Nancy burst onto the street in time to see Ace Burlington's battered patrol car pull away from the curb. White Lightning is parked in a NO PARKING ZONE nearby. A fresh-faced ROOKIE COP stands with one foot on its fender, writing a ticket. He doesn't react as Doc and Ricky clamber into the car.

> NANCY
>
> Take me with you.

> DOC
>
> I'm sorry, Nurse Wallace... but that's impossible.
> This is a two-seater.

He holds up his handcuffed hand, to indicate he's got to take Ricky. Impulsively, she flings her arms around him. She kisses him passionately. Doc squirms, tries to speak through the kiss. Breathless, they both come up for air.

> NANCY
>
> Call me Nancy.

> DOC
>
> N-Nancy... please... not in front of the boy...

Nancy breaks the clinch. She and Doc glance at Ricky, embarrassed. Ricky is hugely disappointed with Doc.

> NANCY
>
> I... I'm sorry. You're so heroic. It makes me crazy.

> DOC
> (struggling for self-control)
> Stay here. Keep an eye on Lanton ... and another one on Chislewit. Remember, one of them must be The Thunder.

> NANCY
> (gently socks his jaw)
> Go get 'em, you big lug.

Doc returns the affectionate sock, snapping Nancy's head around. Then he puts White Lightning into gear and ROARS OFF. The Rookie is left with his foot in mid-air, ticket in hand.

INT. WHITE LIGHTNING - DAY
Doc drives in hot pursuit of Ace's car, the best he can handcuffed to Ricky. Ricky is disgusted.

> RICKY
> You've got lipstick on your goggles.

> CROSS-WIPE TO:

INT. ICARUS AIRCRAFT OFFICE - OUTER HALL - DAY
Rubbing her jaw, Nancy approaches the door, a frosted-glass window with *ICARUS AIRCRAFT COMPANY* written in gold leaf. Suddenly, from within the room, the SOUND OF TWO CONKS ON THE HEAD are heard, each followed by the SOUND OF A FALLING BODY. Nancy rushes forward, flings open the door. Reacts.

> NANCY
> You!

A HISS O.S., and a CLOUD OF GAS surrounds her. She sways, narcotized, and falls to the floor, unconscious.

NANCY'S OUTSTRETCHED HAND

A familiar black-robed figure approaches. CAMERA PANS UP the figure's legs and torso, to arrive at the head as The Thunder settles his mask about his shoulders. He cackles madly.

                                                    IRIS WIPE TO:

EXT. CITY OUTSKIRTS – DAY

Ace's patrol car speeds by, followed after a few beats by White Lightning.

Gams stares, bored, out the window as Ace rattles on.

                          ACE
          ... so then there was the time Dick Tracy had Flat-
          Top pinned down in a cabin out in the woods. Flat-
          Top had Junior prisoner, see, and Tracy couldn't...

The wrist WALKIE-TALKIE SQUAWKS to life.

                    WALKIE-TALKIE
          Calling Ace Burlington. Come in, Inspector Bur-
          lington.

                          ACE
          That's for me.

He swacks himself in the forehead with the walkie-talkie. Gams reacts, grabbing the wheel with one hand, Ace's gun with the other. Ace recovers to find himself covered by Gams.

                          GAMS
          You gotta get a smaller two-way wrist radio, copper.
                       (fiercely)
          Drive where I tell you. Just drive.

                          133

EXT. CITY OUTSKIRTS – DAY

Ace's car makes a sharp turn. White Lightning follows. A beat... and in the next moment. The Thunderwagon rumbles past, moving up fast behind White Lightning.

The Thunder is at the wheel, humming "*Das Valkyrie*," Nurse Nancy bound and gagged, just waking up beside him–reacts, struggles in vain to escape. Thunderwagon RUMBLES. The Thunder closes a knife-switch on his dashboard marked *FRONT GUN*.

THUNDERWAGON'S FRONT GRILL

The grill grinds open, and a Catling Gun thrusts out.

WHITE LIGHTNING

Ricky pulls the notepad from his pocket. He opens it for Doc.

>   RICKY
>   Doc, I just remembered. I found this back in that of-
>   fice. One of Mr. Hooper's notepads. It might be a
>   clue.

THE NOTEPAD

Page upon page, one word written over and over and over: "*SCRIBBLE SCRIBBLE SCRIBBLE*" (etc.)

Doc reacts to this–as GUNFIRE RATTLES behind them. He looks back.

DOC'S POV - THE THUNDERWAGON comes roaring through the dust, CATLING GUN BLASTING away from its front grill.

Ricky whoops with delight.

                    RICKY
          Oh, boy! It's the Thunderwagon!

                    DOC
          We're sitting ducks, as long as I've only got one hand
          free.

Ricky bites his lip, then brings forth the key to the handcuffs.

                    RICKY
          Uh... would this help, Doc?

Doc takes the keys, resisting the temptation to brain Ricky.

                    DOC
          Yes, Ricky. Yes, I really think it would. Yes.

THUNDERWAGON GRILL - CATLING GUN BLASTING away.

REAR OF WHITE LIGHTNING - being peppered with holes by the BULLETS.

Doc finishes freeing himself, hurriedly pulls a lever beside his seat.

WHITE LIGHTNING - THE REAR HOOD folds up, like a shield, between the front seat and the Thunderwagon's GUN-FIRE. BULLETS stitch a pattern across the metal, SPLAT-TERING harmlessly.

Doc twists a knob on the dashboard. A metal tube extends up from the center of the steering wheel, with an eye-piece like a periscope at the end. Doc puts a goggled eye to the eyepiece.

WHITE LIGHTNING'S REAR LICENSE PLATE - The peri-scope lens is visible in the 0 in DYNAMO.

<u>DOC'S POV</u> - THE THUNDERWAGON still BLASTING away.

Frustrated, The Thunder yanks the wheel hard to the right, gears up through ten gears in a complicated shift pattern, and puts his foot down on the gas. He and Nancy are thrown back against their seats as the car surges forward with a LOUD RUMBLE ROAR.

<u>HELICOPTER SHOT - CITY OUTSKIRTS ROAD</u>
The city has been left far behind. The Thunderwagon over-takes White Lightning, passing on the right, traveling at fantastic speed. Ace's car is out front of both.

Gams double-takes in the rearview mirror, looks back over her shoulder at the car-to-car battle behind. Ace continues to drive, nervously watching Gams' gun, which is stuck deep in his belly.

The Thunder laughs as his car comes abreast of White Lightning. He closes another knife switch marked LEFT FLAMETHROWER.

THUNDERWAGON'S LEFT SIDE - The running board swings up, revealing a row of nozzles that spout flame at White Lightning.

WHITE LIGHTNING - swings to the left, as fires spurt along its right fender.

Ricky ducks back as flame shoots up along the passenger door. Doc twists another knob.

WHITE LIGHTNING - THE HOOD ORNAMENT turns on its mounting, and shoots a spray of water over the front end of the car, dousing the flames–

–and soaking Ricky in the process. Doc adjusts the knob–

The hood ornament turns again, sending a more concentrated stream of water into the Thunderwagon's open window.

The Thunder coughs and chokes, hit full in the face by the water stream. He slams his foot on the gas pedal.

HELICOPTER SHOT - CITY OUTSKIRTS ROAD
The Thunderwagon pulls in front of White Lightning. Ace Burlington's car is still ahead of both vehicles.

Gams still watches the rear window. Ace starts to make a grab for Gams' gun, thinking her attention is on the cars behind them.

>   GAMS
>   Don't even think about it.

Ace swallows heavily, moves his hand back to the wheel.

The Thunder, mopping his wet face with a black sleeve, chuckles with delight as he reaches for a knife-switch marked *NAILS*.

THUNDERWAGON'S TRUNK DOOR- snaps up, and a shower of three-penny nails erupts from the trunk.

THE NAILS scatter on the roadway, as White Lightning's tires tear over them with a POP-POP-POP O.S.

The Thunder laughs, as Nancy looks horrified at the side-view mirror.

<u>HER POV</u> - SIDEVIEW MIRROR shows the White Lightning veering across the road, tires blown. It stalls out in the opposite lane, facing oncoming traffic.

WHITE LIGHTNING sits in the road, as a large truck barrels toward it, head-on.

LIGHTNING'S TIRES are flat, the car is on the rims.

Ricky gapes at the oncoming truck.

>   RICKY
>   Doc. Do something, Doc.

Doc pulls a plunger marked *ROBOT ELECTRO-INFLATER* (*For Use In Emergencies Only*).

WHITE LIGHTNING'S FRONT LEFT FENDER - a door opens in the fender, and a robot arm comes out holding an airhose.

<u>INTERCUT</u>:

THE OTHER FENDERS - doors open in quick succession, other robot arms extruding.

THE AIRHOSES - attach to the tires, reinflating them at impossible speed.

THE TIRES - rise one after the other, lifting White Lightning.

THE TRUCK - rushes head-on toward White Lightning.

WIDER
On its re-inflated tires, White Lightning peels out of the path of the barreling truck, narrowly misses it–then recrosses the road and takes off at full speed toward the Thunderwagon, up

ahead. Further on, Ace's car turns onto a road toward the waterfront.

EXT. WATERFRONT ROAD
The three cars head down a foggy waterfront street, toward the wharf area, at high speed.

TRAVELING SHOT - WATERFRONT ROAD
Heavy fog. Ahead, a wharf comes INTO VIEW... and at the end of the wharf, The Thunder's shack/secret headquarters. Ace's car roars down the wharf, followed by Thunderwagon, FIRING away at White Lightning.

Ace trying to see through the fog.

ACE'S POV - THE SHACK, coming up fast. He yells.

INT. THUNDER'S SECRET LAB – DAY
The wall of the lab bursts inward as Ace's patrol car CRASHES through from outside. Shortie and Longjohn, standing by the Rocketplane engine prototype, duck as shards of wood fly past them. Ace's car is followed half a second later by the Thunderwagon and White Lightning, which ram into the rear of Ace's car. Wood and dust and plaster and metal crash down.

Ace and Gams stumble from their car. Ace looks around groggily at Shortie and Longjohn who rush past him with Tommyguns in hand–

ACE
OK, you guys are under arrest!

Shortie and Longjohn ignore Ace as they rush past the Thunderwagon to White Lightning. Shortie runs up–smack into the driver's door–as Doc careens into Longjohn and they crash backward, dropping their Tommyguns, both unconscious.

The Thunder's hands grab up Longjohn's fallen Tommygun. He swings it up, FIRING a burst at–

–Doc, who springs from White Lightning, somersaulting away from the car as Tommygun FIRE churns up the wreckage aroung him. He completes his somersault, landing behind an equipment console.

The Thunder jumps down from the wrecked Thunderwagon, using Longjohn's face as a stepping stone to an uncluttered part of the floor. He looks around, sees Gams shoving Ace away from the patrol car.

                    THUNDER
          Forget him... find Dynamo!

Gams cracks Ace over the head with her gun butt. Ace tries to keep his feet a moment–goes down like a log.

Gams takes off, around the far end of the console, as The Thunder heads round the near end.

Ricky peeks his head up over White Lightning's crumpled dash.

Nancy is still struggling with her bonds in the wrecked Thunderwagon. Ricky helps her slice the ropes on her wrists on a jagged piece of dashboard, pulls off her gag.

The Thunder, closing in on the console, FIRES a burst from his Tommygun until the GUN CLICKS empty. He comes around one end–face to face with Gams at the other end. No sign of Doc. They stare at each other and hear a RATTLING SOUND above. They look up–

TRAVELING SHOT

140

Doc swings down from the balcony, clinging to a set of chains strung across the breadth of the lab. He's taken his belt off and holds it across the chains, riding the resulting sling. His feet crash into The Thunder, knocking him head over heels.

Gams has him in her sights, but can't bring herself to fire.

Doc makes it to the other side of the lab, dropping from view behind the HUMMING TURBINE.

The Thunder is sprawled on the ground, inches from Ace. He and Ace stir awake simultaneously. As Ace blinks at Thunder groggily, Thunder punches Ace out again and scrambles to his feet.

Gams, with a cigarette between her lips, bends to light a match on her stocking. She sees another pair of female legs in front of her–looks up slowly–it's Nurse Nancy, fist cocked. Before Gams can move, Nancy punches her back into the equipment console. Gams' pistol falls onto the console. Nancy goes for it–but Gams, recovering, yanks her off balance to the floor. The gun falls with them, still inches from them as they struggle.

BEHIND TURBINE
Doc and The Thunder are in full battle, trading blows. Doc gets a roundhouse through The Thunder's guard–and it connects with a METALLIC CLANG. His hand hurt, Doc is caught by surprise by The Thunder's follow-up punch, and is knocked sprawling into the turbine.

CLOSE - TURBINE SWITCHES are struck by Doc's shoulder. Lights flash, TURBINE HUMS louder.

The turbine begins to CRACKLE with out-of-control electricity. Sparks of electricity spray about the room, a menace to everybody.

The Thunder sees this, alarmed, and runs for the ladder leading up to the balcony. He has scaled it nearly to the top when—

CLOSE - THUNDER'S BOOTED FOOT is grabbed by Doc's hand from below.

Doc, on the ladder, yanks The Thunder's foot—and it comes off in his hand, revealing metal struts, straps and braces dangling from the end of the boot. Doc gapes at it a moment, then tosses it aside and scrambles up the rest of the ladder onto the balcony.

The Thunder, hopping on one foot, the other foot invisible under his robes, reaches a small trapdoor in the wall marked *EMERGENCY EXIT* in English and Gothic-lettered German. He starts to push through the trapdoor.

Behind him, Doc nimbly sidesteps a low fork of lightning and over-takes The Thunder. Doc's hands latch onto him from behind and swing him around.

Doc punches The Thunder once, twice, three times... and Thunder goes down.

As electricity sparks dangerously all around them, Nancy punches Gams away, and, rolling, grabs the gun, comes up with it aimed at Gams at point-blank range.

Doc lifts Thunder to his feet, but Thunder is laughing maniacally. TURBINE HUMS louder and louder O.S., as electricity sprays the chamber.

                    THUNDER
        You think you've won? Listen, fool—

The turbine shakes on its mounting, electric arcs sparking.

> THUNDER (O.S.)
> –the generator is out of control!

Thunder cackles madly. Doc glances down into the lab, spots Ricky by the Rocketplane engine. The engine is aimed roughly at the sparking generator.

> THUNDER
> You've won nothing but a quick death! The great Doc Dynamo–killed by a dynamo!

Doc knocks him down almost absently.

> DOC
> This is no time for irony.
> (yells down)
> Ricky! The Rocketplane engine–

Ricky glances at the Rocketplane engine...

> DOC (O.S.)
> –turn it on, lad! Turn it on!

Ricky finally gets it. He puts his finger on the red *START* button...

The Thunder reacts with shock.

Nancy and Gams gape.

Inspector Ace gets groggily to his feet and looks around dumbly.

                         ACE
          You're all under–

Ricky's finger pushes the button–

CROSSCUT – And the ROCKETPLANE ENGINE ROARS
to life with terrific force... and soars across the lab into the
turbine–EXPLODING in a blinding burst of light.

EXT. THE THUNDER'S SHACK – DAY
The shack EXPLODES with terrific SOUND and fury. The
blazing Rocketplane engine hurls through the shack roof and
out to sea.

EXT. UNDERSEA - DAY
STOCK FOOTAGE of Nazi sub. Appropriate SOUND EF-
FECTS.

EXT. SKY & SEA - DAY
The blazing Rocketplane engine crashes into the sea... Next
moment, there is a terrific UNDERWATER EXPLOSION as
the sub goes up as well.

                              WIPE TO:

EXT. WATERFRONT SHORE – DAY
Police CARS, SIRENS HOWLING, SCREECH to a stop near
the shore, where bits of lab debris have washed up. Out of a
third car pour several reporters with cameras and notepads.
Prominent among the wreckage... several coughing, half-
drowned figures: Ricky, Nancy, Ace, Gams, Shortie and
Longjohn.

                         ACE
          Put the cuffs on these jokers.

He indicates the crooks, whom the cops take into custody. Ace turns, grinning proudly, to the reporters.

> ACE (cont'd)
> The name's Burlington, boys. Inspector Arthur Burlington. Call me Ace.

Doc and the Thunder come out of the surf, Doc hauling Thunder by the hem of his long robe. Thunder's feet drag in the sand... revealing six-inch thick "elevator" shoes. Doc pulls Thunder to his feet as Nancy and Ricky crowd around.

> NANCY
> Doc! You're alive! And you've got The Thunder!

> THUNDER
> (coughing, choking)
> Could we talk about this?

> DOC
> You and we have nothing to talk about, Thunder. Or should I call you by your real name–
> (yanks the mask from Thunder's head)
> –Stanley Hooper!

The tattered robe falls away, revealing Hooper in a heavy metal exo-skeleton, like football padding, as well as elevator shoes. Doc pulls Hooper's soggy notepad from his own belt.

> DOC (cont'd)
> I believe this is yours.

Hooper takes it meekly. A cop drags Hooper/Thunder away.

> NANCY
> (hugging Doc's arm)
> This is so exciting.

DOC

It's a proud day for democracy, Nurse Wallace...

NANCY

Nancy, remember?

DOC

I mean... Nancy.
(emboldened)
I'm just sorry we couldn't have rescued the Rocketplane engine, as well as ourselves.

ACE

Hey, that's right! And with Keppler and Palmer both
dead...

NANCY

The Rocketplane will have to remain a fantastic
dream.

DOC

(thoughtful, looks to sky)
Imagine... with an entire fleet of Rocketplanes pa-
trolling the sky, America need never have feared an
enemy attack, from land or sea.

RICKY

Until somebody else came up with a faster plane,
anyway,
(shaking sand from a shoe)
Say, Doc, this was the most fun yet! Next week, can
we take on some Panzer tanks?

NANCY

Ricky, just once... will you please shut up?

Doc, Nancy and Ace look at each other... and slowly... with Doc joining last... they start laughing. Ricky looks sullen... then smirks... and starts laughing, too. Laughing so hard he can barely stand up as we

CUT TO:

NEWSREEL LOGO (BLACK & WHITE) - "*MOVIETOWN NEWS*"

Briefly on the screen. TITLE CARD (WITH *MOVIETOWN NEWS* LOGO). It reads: "*HEROIC POLICE INSPECTOR CAPTURES TOP ENEMY SPY!*"

NEWSREEL SHOTS (B&W, EDITED FROM ABOVE SEQUENCE) of a smiling Ace Burlington surrounded by reporters, police, as The Thunder is taken away. The usual UPBEAT MUSIC.

NARRATOR
This is the one that didn't get away from Inspector Arthur "Ace" Burlington as he turns The Thunder, Adolph Hitler's top American spy, over to Bigtown police.
(swell of MUSIC)
Our hero didn't neglect to spread the credit around, though, as he generously acknowledged the assistance of the masked man of mystery known only as... Doc Dynamo.

One-second INSERT of Doc Dynamo, then back to Ace with reporters.

<u>TITLE CARD</u> (WITH LOGO). It reads: "*GAMS CATLING MOB SENT UP FOR 99 YEARS!*"

NEWSREEL FOOTAGE (B&W) - GAMS, SHORTIE, & LONGJOHN behind bars, in prison stripes, looking glum. Gams has already modified her outfit into a sexy skirt, slit up the sides, etc., and is straightening a seam as she flirts with an obviously mesmerized prison guard.

> NARRATOR
> In a related story, The Thunder's henchmen, Gams Catling and her gang, were sentenced to 99 consecutive terms of one year each for treason and loitering with intent to do bodily harm.

NEWSREEL FOOTAGE (B&W) - DR. FRED & NANCY beaming, in their office. Both wear their medical outfits.

> NARRATOR
> Finally, in society news, Dr. Fred Franklin, well-known East Coast pediatrician to the rich and wealthy, announced his engagement to his nurse, Miss Nancy Wallace.

Nancy holds up huge engagement ring which sparkles like hell.

Suddenly, Ricky enters the scene carrying Doc Dynamo's helmet, goggles and flight suit.

Dr. Fred, still smiling determinedly, shoves a wad of dollar bills into Ricky's hand. Ricky mouths a "Gosh, thanks, Dr. Fred" and rushes off as Dr. Fred and Nancy hurriedly sit on the Doc Dynamo costume.

NARRATOR (cont'd)
The couple has announced wedding plans for some-
time in the late 1950s.

NEWSREEL LOGO (B&W) - "*MOVIETOWN NEWS*"
An invisible hand writes the words "THE END" across the
logo, MUSIC SWELLS, and we

FADE OUT.

THE END

ABOUT THE AUTHORS

Gerry CONWAY is the creator of dozens of popular comic book characters, among them *The Punisher*, *Steel* and *Firestorm* (all adapted to film and television) and is perhaps best known in comics as "The Man Who Killed Gwen Stacy." (The first *Spider-Man* movie was adapted in part from this story.) His novels *The Midnight Dancers* and *Mindship* are available in e-book format from Embid Publishing. His film credits include *Conan the Destroyer* and *Fire and Ice*. In television, he has been a Consulting Producer for *Hercules: The Legendary Journeys*, Executive Producer of *The Huntress* and currently, Co-Executive Producer of *Law & Order: Criminal Intent*. As a television writer, Gerry has been nominated for several Emmys, and his teleplay *Conscience* was nominated for the Mystery Writers of America's Edgar Award in 2004.

Roy THOMAS has been a comic book writer (and often editor) since 1965, primarily for Marvel and DC. He was editor-in-chief of Marvel Comics from 1972 to 1974, and is particularly noted for his scripting of *Conan the Barbarian*, *The Avengers*, *X-Men*, *The Incredible Hulk*, *The Invaders*, *All-Star Squadron* and *Infinity, Inc.* In 2004-2005, for Marvel, Roy finished an adaptation, begun in 1974, of Bram Stoker's *Dracula*. In a major poll in the late 1990s, he was voted by pros and fans the fourth favorite editor and fifth favorite comic book writer of the 20th century. Between 1980-2000, Roy co-wrote and sold nine screenplays, of which two (*Conan the Destroyer* and *Fire and Ice*) were made into films. In addition to scripting comics, Roy continues to chronicle the medium's history in his acclaimed monthly magazine *Alter Ego*.

www.ingramcontent.com/pod-product-compliance
Lightning Source LLC
Chambersburg PA
CBHW030519260626
47157CB00005B/1803